VALLEY OF THE LAWLESS

Matt Landry is to marry Adriane Driscoll, daughter of the man who runs the huge Target Cattle Company. Riding through the Wyoming Territory, Matt witnesses a couple being ambushed by masked riders. He comes to the aid of the survivor, Bonnie McClain, and is appalled when she tells him the attackers were from Target. Now both he and Bonnie, as witnesses to her husband's murder, are in constant danger. As the trouble escalates in the valley, Matt must choose sides . . .

Books by M. Lemartine
in the Linford Western Library:

MAVERICK GUN

M. LEMARTINE

VALLEY OF THE LAWLESS

Complete and Unabridged

LINFORD
Leicester

First published in the
United States of America

First Linford Edition
published 2000

All characters in this book are fictitious,
and any resemblance to actual persons,
living or dead, is purely coincidental

British Library CIP Data

Lemartine, M.
Valley of the lawless.—Large print ed.—
Linford western library
1. Western stories
2. Large type books
I. Title
823.9′14 [F]

ISBN 0–7089–5624–6

Published by
F. A. Thorpe (Publishing) Ltd.
Anstey, Leicestershire

Set by Words & Graphics Ltd.
Anstey, Leicestershire
Printed and bound in Great Britain by
T. J. International Ltd., Padstow, Cornwall

This book is printed on acid-free paper

With love to my beautiful,
delightful nieces, Cheryl, Dena,
Diana, Kathy, and Leann,
and to my handsome,
rough-and-ready nephews,
Donald, Duane, and Jack

M. Lemartine is a pseudonym of Lee Martin, who also writes as Lee Samuel and Lee Phillips.

1

The sound of gunfire echoed in the green hills of northern Wyoming Territory. Matt Landry reined his blue-roan horse to a halt and reached for his Winchester, drawing it from the scabbard. He listened intently, his grey-blue eyes shadowed by the wide brim of his black Stetson.

His big frame was tense, his hard square jaw jutting as he looked slowly in all directions. The cool afternoon breeze was rustling his dark brown hair, cropped to his collar. His leather jacket and vest were suddenly too warm.

Again the shots rang out. They came from the north, where the distant blue mountains were draped in a mist against rising dark clouds.

New to this part of the territory, Matt was not yet aware that two years ago in 1876 Custer had met his defeat only seventy miles north of where he was now riding. Ranches and settlements were widely scattered in this newly opened range, and trouble could descend on him at any second.

The creak of his saddle leather had never been so loud, the smell of his horse's sweat never so strong. He worked the lever on his Winchester, sending a shell into the chamber that seemed to ring across the land.

Matt turned his gelding toward the echo of the gunfire and rested his repeater on the pommel. In his early thirties, he rode easy in the saddle. But he was weary, not having slept well for all of the nights enroute. He had ridden over two hundred miles north from Cheyenne to be married, despite his misgivings.

As he rode up a grade he discovered he was on a cliff. He looked north up the deep, rocky canyon lined with high walls crested with dark pine. A wide, busy stream was running fast and swift through the rocks hundreds of feet below.

He heard the gunfire once more. Then he saw it on the far side to his right: a spring wagon racing along the edge of the ridge, fighting to avoid the terrible plunge.

Matt reached in his saddlebag and drew out the army spyglass he had carried for years. He held it to his right eye and adjusted it.

A man with a woman wearing a shawl around her head were on the wagon seat along with a large black dog bouncing in the bed on barrels and boxes. Crowding the wagon were a dozen riders, shooting and cracking whips. The man was holding back on the reins as the wagon raced along the rim, but the riders were whipping his horses to higher speed and driving them closer to the edge of the cliff. Now the driver was firing back at them.

Suddenly, the man grabbed at his face and was knocked back over the seat into the bed with the crazed dog.

His team veered to his left and ran right off the edge.

Helpless and out of range, Matt could only stare as the wagon hovered in space like some giant bug. The team of bays fought the air struggling and kicking as they fell, carrying the wagon with them.

The woman's scream echoed along the canyon walls.

Matt started down a steep deer trail, unable to tear his gaze from the falling wagon. It seemed an eternity as it bounced off the canyon walls for several hundred feet, then continued in wild disarray another hundred feet toward the bottom.

The horses crashed into brush along the cliff wall. The woman was propelled off the wagon and thrown on top of them like a rag doll, falling the rest of the way on the back of one of them. The dog rode the wagon until it broke apart, throwing the animal wildly toward the creek, while the man's body rolled into the grass.

Matt reined up in the cover of the brush, watching the dust rise around the horrible destruction. He saw the riders watch for signs of life for some time before they turned and disappeared from the cliff's edge.

His mouth dry and stomach churning, Matt returned his spyglass to the saddlebag. He rode the dangerous path all the way down into the canyon and headed up the creek. The woman's scream was still echoing in his ears. No one could have survived that fall.

When he came on the scene, he reined up.

The wagon had smashed into pieces that were thrown in all directions, along with luggage and barrels of flour and other supplies. The dead man lay in the grass near the creek. He appeared to be a rancher in his forties, wearing a Sunday-go-meeting coat and string tie.

The dog was in the water, fighting the current, its white nose pointed upward. The creek was some fifteen feet across and set with rocks and branches.

The woman had landed on the horses, then rolled into the grass some eighty feet further up the canyon. Wearing a blue cape and white dress, she lay still as death. Her golden hair gleamed in the morning sunlight, and her face was turned away from him. The dead horses were in the rocks above her.

Matt dismounted, leaving his roan ground-tied, and walked over to the dead man. A bullwhip had cut his face and throat, strangling him before he ever left the wagon seat — an accident perhaps, or cold-blooded murder.

Turning, he saw that the black dog was caught by rocks and tangled in floating branches and was sinking fast, its white nose barely above water, white paws clawing at the surface. It was a miracle it was alive, and Matt needed to find something alive before he wept.

'Hold on, fella,' Matt shouted.

He unbuckled his gun belt and waded into the deep swirling water. The current went up to his waist, and he was fighting it as he caught the animal by the back of the neck. He freed it from the debris and started pulling it back toward shore. As he fought the fierce water and slippery bottom he began to wonder if he was going to make it.

With great effort he staggered out of the raging current, jerking the big dog with him. As he collapsed on the wet bank the animal dropped to its belly nearby. Its eerie brown eyes gleamed as it growled at Matt.

'Hey, it wasn't me,' Matt said, breathing hard.

The animal flashed its teeth, curling its lips back.

Matt struggled to his feet. He was chilled through, but he pulled on his six-gun and walked through the debris from the wagon. He picked up some blankets and covered the dead man, then walked over to the woman. He would have to bury them both. The horses were dead, and there was no easy way to get the bodies out of the canyon.

As he knelt he saw the glitter of sunlight in her flaxen hair. It lay in great waves about her pretty white face. Her eyes were closed under long lashes. Under her torn cape she was wearing a white lacey outfit that looked like a wedding dress. She looked to be in her mid-twenties. In a sad moment of thought he reached to stroke her left cheek. She was still warm but lifeless. Uneasy, he draped a blanket over her.

As he slid his hands beneath her and started to lift her from the grass he heard a moan and found himself staring into large, blue-green eyes. They gazed at him unseeingly as her lips parted.

He drew back. 'Thank goodness, you're alive.'

'My husband?' she whispered.

'He didn't make it.'

'I hurt so bad.'

'Do you feel anything in your legs?'

'I'm not sure.'

Fighting tears of joy that she was

alive, he was on his knees as he inched down past her hips. He put his hands on her through the white dress and layers of petticoat, pressing down on her thighs.

'Feel that?'

'Yes.'

'Can you wiggle your toes? How about your fingers?'

She nodded as she fought for new breath.

He returned to kneel near her waist. 'I'm going to carry you down to the creek. If anything hurts too much, holler.'

She moaned as he slid his hands beneath her and lifted as gently as he could. He drew her up into his arms and staggered to his feet, trying not to hurt her. She was surprisingly light as her head rolled against his chest, her flaxen hair about her face.

He carried her over near the dog, which had sniffed the man's body and then retreated to where Matt had left it. He set her down on another blanket, then pulled it up around her as she lay on her back. She was gazing at him with more clarity.

'It was Target riders,' she murmured.

Matt sat back on his heels, startled. He had come all this way to marry Adriane Driscoll, a sweet and lovely young woman whose father ran the huge Target Cattle Company near Wrangler.

'How do you know that?' he asked.

'They had bandannas over their faces, but Will said they were from Target.'

He drew her blanket up more closely and touched her soft hair to spread it from her face. 'For now, you just rest.'

'Will was whipped around his eyes. That's why we went off the cliff.'

'Whoever they are, they might come back. I'll bury your husband as best I can, then make a travois and try to get us away from here. We'll camp down the canyon.'

'Please, a marker, a cross.'

'Later. Right now, the game is survival.'

As he stood up he paused to stare down at her as she spread the blanket and cape to touch the lace on the front of her dress, fingering it with her eyes closed.

He reached down to cover her with the blanket once more and set about with the unpleasant task of burial. He used a shovel from the wagon and made the grave close to the foot of the ridge and covered it with brush. He whispered a prayer with tears brimming.

Then, using parts of the wagon and some of the rope from the supplies, he made a travois. The woman again moaned when he moved her, and he feared that she might have broken bones or internal bleeding. He tied her on the travois with some of the supplies and led his horse back down the canyon, out of sight of the ridge. The big dog trailed, still wary of him.

Clouds were darkening the sky, and it

was early evening when he stopped. The canyon was narrower, but the ridge overhang gave protection from anyone riding above. He unsaddled and tethered his roan. He made camp in a hollow of the cliff wall and built a fire in a circle of rocks, using brush and some cow chips. Soon the flames were blazing hot with stench.

The dog lay nearby, watching.

The woman rested in her blankets, tears trickling down her face as the shock slowly left her. Now she was wracked with pain and sadness. Matt knelt to give her water from his canteen while waiting for the coffee to brew in the big iron pot he had salvaged.

'I had just met Will McClain,' she said, softly. 'It was arranged by mail. His wife had been killed a year ago when he first got here. I came in on the stage yesterday, and we were married this morning in Wrangler. My name is Bonnie, Bonnie McClain.'

'Matt Landry.'

She wiped tears from her face. 'The

delegate to Washington?'

He nodded. 'But I gave that up.'

'You don't look like a lawyer. You look like some drifting cowboy. Or a gunfighter.'

'You ain't far off. My brothers are all lawmen, and I reckon I feel better out here with a six-gun than back in Cheyenne with a suit you can't sit down in. But listen, do you think you can eat? There's coffee and some hardtack. And I saw some beans in one of those sacks.'

'I'll try some coffee.'

'You get any sign you're bleedin' internally or if anything's broken, you let me know right off.'

He poured hot coffee for her and held it close.

She rose on her elbow and took the cup in her trembling hand, sipping it slowly and closing her eyes for a moment. Then she lay back, the cup at her side.

Matt threw the dog some hardtack. It hesitated, pulled the bread between its front paws, and sniffed it, but it didn't eat a bite.

'He sure is careful,' Matt said.

'Will said he got him from some medicine show man who was going to jail for stealing from the crowds. He said Blackie was trained to steal things from people, but he didn't want Blackie shot, so he took him.'

'Sounds like he was a good man.'

She closed her eyes, biting her lip. 'Will's family is really going to be hurt. The attack was so brutal.'

'Do you think your husband hit any of 'em?'

'I don't know. It was all happening so fast. They had chased us for a long time, whipping our horses. They were firing into the air, not at us. But when we got close to the cliff, Will got afraid and started shooting. That's when they turned the whip on him.'

By the light of the flickering campfire he fed her beans and hardtack, but she could barely swallow. Matt admired her pretty features, her small turned-up nose, and the way her eyes glistened in the firelight like crystal. Tears were still trickling down her face.

'What made you come out here? I mean, a good-looking woman like you could have had anyone. Why marry a stranger?'

She flushed. 'It's a long story. What about you? Why did you get involved in politics when all your brothers were lawmen?'

'I guess I was the black sheep all right.'

That brought a smile to her face. 'And why did you come this far north?'

'Have some more coffee.'

She gazed at him curiously, but she was too tired to care. She lay back in her blankets, moving carefully. He knelt to cover her, resting his hand on her burning face. She allowed a flickering smile to cross her lips, then closed her eyes and fell asleep.

Matt chewed on some hardtack but had no appetite. He watched over her for hours as she moaned in her sleep, keeping the fire hot as the chill of night settled in. He listened to the rushing, icy stream some sixty feet away and down a slope.

He thought of Adriane and how he had met her in Cheyenne at a party for the governor. She had worn blue silk and was charming everyone there, including Matt, who had been lonely. He had been startled when she had turned her attention on him, and before he knew it they were making plans.

'You'll love Father,' she had said. 'And my brother, Kerby. They have one of the largest cattle companies in Wyoming Territory. And someday you'll share in it, Matt, but right now you have to make all the right contacts. I have to go stay with them now, but when you come we'll be married and head right back to Cheyenne.'

Matt had squirmed when she and the governor made political plans for him extending far beyond being a delegate in the fight for statehood. Yet he had been so enamored of her that she could have led him anywhere.

'Don't worry, Matt,' Adriane had said in the shadows one night. 'Father will back you all the way to the governor's seat.'

Matt had been flattered, but now he just shook his head. Staring into the flickering flames, he thought of ways to tell her that here was where he wanted to be. Here the stars filled the sky at night, more glorious than any glitter in Cheyenne or Washington. And here a man could ride free in the wind and wear leather and buckskin.

Out here, however, there was danger from marauding Sioux and Cheyenne. But there were elk and deer, pronghorns and cottontails, wolves and coyotes, grizzlies in the mountains, fish in the streams. Sometimes, a man could stumble on roaming herds of buffalo and perch on a rock, watching them pass all day. And there was grass everywhere for a man's herd. She was a rancher's daughter. She would understand.

At length he slept off and on, sitting

up against a rock. His rifle lay across his knees, his blankets around him. A chunk of hardtack was still on his plate next to a cold cup of coffee near his feet.

He sensed something moving near him and carefully peered from under his hat brim. The dog had sneaked around the campfire and was closing in on him. It lapped Matt's coffee from the cup. Matt grinned but remained still, eyes nearly closed. It sniffed Matt's plate and then carefully seized the hardtack with its teeth and backed away. Its eyes gleamed in the pale light as it waited for Matt to move. Then it turned and trotted back to where the other chunk of hardtack still lay in the grass. It was Matt's he wanted. Matt grinned, and he slept a little more.

Soon it was raining hard and persistently. They were sheltered by the cliff, and the dog came in out of the rain. It wouldn't come near the fire as long as Matt was watching it. Lightning flashed, and the rain became so heavy it was loud and droning, beating the ground and rushing silt to the creek below. Matt slept fitfully.

He awakened just as dawn was breaking. The dog was in the deep grass, growling softly. The fire had died down, and Matt rose to one knee, letting his blankets fall from around him. Bonnie was still asleep. The rain was only a drizzle now.

He heard horses coming down the canyon and kicked dirt over the fire.

2

Matt knew the rocks against the canyon wall were little shelter, and the smouldering fire was giving off smoke. He glanced at Bonnie, sleeping soundly with exhaustion as first light glowed on the rocks above and rain continued to drizzle from a dark sky.

The hoofbeats were drawing near, deep thuds on the muddy ground. The dog didn't move but was listening intently.

Rising to stand with his Winchester cocked, Matt swallowed, his throat bone dry. If it was the dozen riders who had covered their faces with bandannas in the fury of their kill, his chances were pretty slim.

Somebody wanted this woman dead. And Matt would die right along with her. He had been a witness.

Coming around the distant corner

along the rushing water were three riders on sorrel horses.

One was an old Apache wearing buckskins under his heavy leather coat. He had grey hair to his shoulders, a face square and weathered, and piercing brown eyes that searched the canyon as he held his rifle across the pommel.

With him was a cowhand in his fifties with an old Stetson, worn and marked with sweat. Wearing a slicker over his ranch clothes, he had a greying handlebar mustache and sat in the saddle like a man who was born to it. He didn't have his rifle pulled as he leaned down to gaze at the grass. They were nearly a hundred feet away.

Keeping pace was a young hand in a slicker with his hat thrown back from the chin strap. His head of pale blond hair was fluffy and unkempt.

The Apache spotted the camp and reined up first. The three men sat in their saddles in silence, gazing at Matt. It was the Apache who was satisfied first and rode forward, the others following.

Matt lowered his rifle as they dismounted.

'Oh no,' the older cowhand said, tears in his eyes. He stood staring at the sleeping woman. 'Is that Mrs. McClain? We thought she had been washed away in the creek.'

'You ride for the McClains?'

'Sure do. Me and young Todd here, and Single-Foot.'

'Single-Foot?'

'Well, he's a real fast runner. Apache.'

'Chiricahua,' the Apache added.

The cowhand nodded. 'He was a scout for the army when Will was in it, down in Arizona Territory, and they stuck together. Me, I'm Jasper Mickleson.'

'Matt Landry.'

Jasper hesitated, his eyes darkening. His mouth twisted down at one corner, and he appeared confused and angry. Yet as Matt stepped forward, they shook hands.

Jasper turned and gazed at the sleeping woman and spoke softly. 'You know, Will was still grievin' over his wife when he got this letter from Missouri. Next thing we knowed, he was gettin' married again. Now she's a widow right off.'

'I was out of range, but I saw them get run off the cliff by a dozen men with their faces covered. It was cold-blooded murder.'

Jasper pulled off his slicker in the shelter of the rocks, then sat back on his heels as Matt built up the fire and put the coffee on the burning chips and brush. The cowhand rubbed his chin and shook his head, his rough face grim.

'This ain't easy country.'

'You got any idea who wanted them dead?'

'I ain't sure, but the Target Cattle Company, run by King Driscoll, is trying to run roughshod over everyone. And Will had a real feud going with young Kerby Driscoll.'

'What about?'

'Somethin' to do with the death of Will's wife.'

'How did she die?'

Before the cowhand could answer, Bonnie stirred and opened her eyes, staring at the visitors. She rose on her elbow, drawing the blankets up around her.

'Mrs. McClain, we're mighty glad you're alive,' Jasper said, then introduced himself and the others.

Matt knelt to pour coffee for everyone as Bonnie slid closer to the fire, keeping her blankets around her. The men sat cross-legged to savor their coffee, except for Single-Foot, who stood aside to watch the canyon trail. Todd had removed his slicker, showing a slight body more skinny than not.

Bonnie spoke softly. 'Will said they were Target riders.'

Jasper shrugged. 'Maybe he was just guessing.'

'The one with the bullwhip, he was laughing when he hit Will across the face and drove us off the cliff. Then he shouted something. It sounded French.'

Jasper became so angry as he listened to her story of the deadly attack that he could not speak for a long while. Then he poured himself some more coffee and turned to her, his concern for her obvious.

'We got worried when you didn't get to the ranch. We had a big supper planned for you and Will. Now, maybe you want to just go on back to Missouri. But if you want to claim title to that there ranch, we'll back you all the way.'

She glanced at the silent Single-Foot and the smiling Todd. Tears filled her eyes and she looked away, holding a coffee cup in both hands as Matt filled it. 'I have no reason to go back.'

'We'll help you all we can,' Jasper told her.

'The first thing is to arrest the men that did this.'

Jasper shrugged. 'We got no proof.'

'I told you. Will knew they were from Target.'

'Driscoll has a lot of men at Target. Do you remember anything else?'

'No. It happened so fast.'

Jasper sipped his coffee. 'Well, I think Matt here will tell you that even if it was Target riders, you got to prove which ones, or you got to prove Driscoll sent 'em.'

She looked up through her tears. 'Are you saying they'll get away free?'

'Well, Ma'am,' Jasper said, 'I'm sayin' what we got ain't enough.'

'Is he right, Matt?'

'Just about.'

She wiped away her angry tears and brushed her long glistening hair from her face. Daylight began to fill the canyon. The clouds thinned, and there were patches of blue sky. They had beans with the rest of the hardtack for breakfast.

The dog wouldn't take food from anyone, and Jasper just shook his head. 'Blackie'd rather steal it. And he'll steal your boot, or your gloves, or anything you turn your back on if he thinks it's important to you.'

'He's pretty smart,' Matt said.

'He could have the makin's of a good cow-dog. But he's already been trained to steal, and Blackie has too much fun at it. He likes gettin' the best of you.'

'I'd like to buy 'im,' Matt said.

Jasper grunted. 'You'd be loco. He can't be trained no more. Look, nobody rewards him for stealin' like that thief must have been doin', but Blackie keeps on sneakin' stuff. You'd think he'd get tired of not gettin' paid off.'

'I'd still like to have him.'

'It's up to Mrs. McClain.'

'Matt saved my life,' she said. 'He can have anything.'

'Don't matter,' said Todd, playing with Matt's spyglass. 'That dog's gonna do what he wants.'

Later, some distance from the camp, Matt rubbed down his roan as Jasper, Todd, and Single-Foot saddled their sorrels. Bonnie was back at the fire, still wrapped in her blankets, and the dog was off in the grass, watching. The morning sun was sprinkling through, but it was cold and damp.

'You comin' to the ranch with us?' Jasper asked Matt.

'No, I got to go into town. That's where I was headed when I heard the shootin'. There a doctor in Wrangler?'

'No, there ain't. The town's hardly a year old. You know they moved the Sioux, Cheyenne, and Arapaho out of here and opened the range in '77. But the Target Cattle Company sneaked in late in '76, six months after Custer got killed. They took over most of the grass between here and the Little Powder River, some hundred miles east of here, before the rest of us could move in.'

'Is there a doctor at Fort McKinney?'

'Might be a surgeon down there, but I ain't sure and it's a two- or three-day ride. We mostly use the barber in town. He had some medical training in the Civil War. But she seems okay now,' he said, indicating Bonnie.

'Keep an eye on her.'

Jasper nodded. 'You know, one of the few around here who can talk French is Kid Monet, a gunman who works for Driscoll and mostly hangs out at the saloon. Now maybe it was him, and maybe it wasn't. Could be they was all just funnin' and tryin' to scare 'em, and maybe they didn't mean to run 'em off the cliff. But Will McClain's dead just the same.'

'It's called reckless disregard of human life.'

'That's them all right.'

'But even if the riders worked for the Driscolls, it doesn't mean the family knew what they were doin',' Matt reasoned.

'You ever in the army, Matt?'

'Yes, I was.'

'Then you know who's got responsibility.'

'From what I heard of Mr. Driscoll, he wouldn't allow that kind of murder.'

'You ever met him?'

'No.'

'Then let me give you a little information. He has a lot of gunmen just like Monet. And he hired Big-Nose George Pollard, an outlaw who used to have a gang around here before we moved in. Then there's Red Oliver, he lives in Pollard's old place. And as for Kerby Driscoll, he ain't no angel.'

'Reckon I'll see for myself.'

'Look here, Matt, we've all heard the rumor you're comin' here to marry Adriane Driscoll. When Mrs. McClain finds out, she won't be thinkin' so kindly of you.'

'What about the law in wrangler?' Matt asked as he set the blanket on his roan.

'Well, there ain't no real law in Pease County, not yet anyhow. The governor says we ain't got enough folks to organize. But we elected a mayor, and he appointed a town sheriff named Gordon. Gordon's always fawnin' over the Driscolls. Always says we don't never have no evidence against Pollard or Target and how he can't do nothin' outside of town.'

Matt put on the saddle and cinched up his roan.

'There's a move to change it from Pease to Johnson County.'

'They're always doin' somethin' we don't need. What we really need around here is a U.S. Marshal. Now Pollard, he went down to Texas for another herd, and he should be back soon. And the only place Target can put more cattle is on McClain's or Oliver's or some of the others.'

'You might need an injunction. Got a judge here?'

'Yeah, a circuit judge, Abnauther. He's got his office in Wrangler.'

Matt dropped the stirrup. 'You might need him.'

'We can't prove nothin', but Target rolled over a half dozen homesteaders like they was prairie dogs.'

'Meaning?'

'They was all found dead.'

Matt swung his saddlebags behind the cantle, then tied down his bedroll and possibles. 'Anyone ever prove who done it?'

'Nope, and listen here, Matt, I know if you marry Miss Driscoll, you'll be ridin' for the brand, but afore you step in that cow puddle, you'd better be knowin' what's there. Watch your step, will you?'

Matt shrugged. 'Thanks.'

Matt turned around to discover the dog had disappeared, perhaps back to Will's grave or just looking for another home. Matt was disappointed.

'Hey, Matt,' said Todd. 'Can I have another look through your spyglass? Looks like an eagle's up there on the ridge.'

Matt nodded and reached in his saddlebags. The spyglass was gone. Irritated, he went back to the camp, looked around, then retraced his steps.

'Where the devil is it?'

'I figure Blackie's gettin' a good view of the country about now,' Jasper said with a grin.

Matt straightened. 'You ain't serious.'

'I told you, that dog will steal anything you make a fuss over. And Todd was playin' with it, so Blackie just figured it was somethin' important. And that's just what he likes.'

'Yeah,' Todd said. 'He ran off with my harmonica, and I got it back, but I ain't played it since, I can tell you that. And he stole Jasper's pipe once.'

'Wait'll I get my hands on him,' Matt said.

Jasper shook his head. 'He's long gone.'

Bonnie left the campfire and came slowly over to them, blankets still around her as she limped on the rough terrain. She was looking prettier and prettier, her large eyes fixed on Matt as she drew the blankets tighter in the morning chill.

'Thank you, Matt Landry.'

Then she stepped forward and came up to him close as she ran her fingers up his chest, sending shivers down his back. She stood on her tiptoes, blankets falling away as she leaned against him and slid her hand around his neck to pull his head down. He was so startled, he couldn't breathe.

Then she planted a honey-sweet kiss on his rough mouth. He felt his knees give way, and his heart was rattling in his chest. He nearly fell backwards as she drew away, still with the soft smile on her lovely face.

Matt was shattered. His stolen kisses with Adriane had been romantic enough. But this kiss had brought a surge of color to his face. Sweat covered him.

'God sent you to help us,' she whispered.

'Don't lift me too high. It's a long way down.'

Matt glanced at the frowning Jasper, who was picking up the blankets to wrap around her once more. It was obvious the cowhand didn't trust Matt, and at this moment Matt couldn't blame him. And Bonnie would hate him when she learned he was to marry a Driscoll.

Matt left them and headed for Wrangler, but on the way he reined up. Blackie was on the rocks ahead, the spyglass clamped in his mouth, tail wagging, rear end in the air as he rested his jaw on his front paws.

'Blast you, give me that.'

Blackie's tail flipped up and down. Matt didn't ride forward but waited, his hand on his lariat. He didn't want to hurt the dog, but he wanted the treasured spyglass.

Blackie set the glass down and sat back, head sideways, watching Matt. Then he barked. Matt allowed his roan to move forward slowly, then reined up within twenty feet.

'You'd better stay right where you are, fella.'

The dog barked again, then spun and ran off through the rocks, vanishing.

Matt rode over, bent down to retrieve the glass, then straightened in the saddle. 'You can come back now.'

But the dog never returned.

Matt tried calling and whistling — nothing.

Annoyed, Matt turned his roan toward Wrangler and forced himself to think of Adriane. It had been months since he had seen her. He was anxious to forget these accusations against Target and to prove to himself Adriane's father was an honorable man. As soon as he was cleaned up, he would be on his way.

* * *

Waiting for him at Target in the large mansion with a few plush furnishings and a young woman for a maid, was Adriane Driscoll. She was in her chambers admiring herself in the ornate wall mirror just shipped in from St. Louis. She twisted and turned in the blue-velvet dress. Light came through the lace curtains.

'What do you think, Lenny?'

'You sure look grand, Miss Adriane.'

'Enough for a governor's lady?'

'You think Mr. Landry will be governor?'

'I know he will. I'll see to it.'

Adriane smiled. Her light brown hair was the color of her eyes. Her oval face with rounded cheekbones turned rosy at her thoughts. She had a fine education, a wealthy father, new clothes, and Matt Landry. Nothing could stop her now.

Dancing down the winding staircase to the parlor with sparce but expensive furniture, she found her father in front of the fireplace with his pipe and a book. He was a heavyset man with thick brows, an irregular nose, a big jaw, and pockmarks; yet he was a handsome man.

'Adriane, I can't believe you're up so early.'

'Father, I just wish the rest of our furniture would arrive. I so need the piano.'

'Don't worry. This will be a show-place, like I promised.'

'But Wrangler's so small, and you

have most of the valley. Who are we going to impress?'

'There'll be plenty of town when we get the railroad up from Casper. We'll take over the whole county. And this Matt Landry, he'd better be the man you say he is. I don't want any trouble from him.'

'He'll be fine,' she said, kissing his cheek, 'and he'll do anything I ask. He's wild about me.'

'He's got those brothers, all lawmen.'

'But they are a long way from here and will not be invited to the wedding if I can help it. Now, I want to give a big dance so I can announce our engagement. And we'll invite governor Hoyt. He's really behind Matt, especially after he learned that Matt studied law under John Kingman, over in Laramie.'

'What about you, honey? Women are voting in this territory and sitting on juries. And some have filed for homesteads. Why not governor?'

'You're teasing me. Matt will be governor. And he won't stop there.'

'That why you fell in love with him?'

'No, of course not.'

'This is your father you're talking to.'

She laughed and sat on the edge of his chair to kiss him again. Then she sobered. 'Matt studied law, but he talks like a cowhand. I want you to work with him on his speech. Make him talk like you.'

'We'll see. Right now, I'm looking forward to a lot of grandchildren.'

She frowned. 'Having babies ruins your figure. And they take all your time. When Matt is governor, I'll be giving teas, and as hostess at parties I'll want to dress with elegance. I just don't want to look like some matron before I'm forty.'

'Does Matt know how you feel about that?'

'Of course not. Now tell me, where is Kerby?'

'Your brother's in town, drinking and gambling as usual.'

She straightened. 'Don't let Kerby ruin things for me. He already forced us out of Tennessee and Ohio, where we were doing so well. If the people in this valley knew what he had done, we'd have to move on again. I couldn't bear it.'

'Nobody's going to find out.'

'What if he does it again?'

'You and I are the only ones who know what he did. And I've had a good talk with him.'

'What if he already has done it again?'

'What are you getting at?'

'I don't know, Father. Just a feeling.'

* * *

While the Driscolls talked quietly, Matt Landry was heading into Wrangler across the open, rolling grasslands dotted with yellow flowers. A dark green creek crossed the trail near the town's eastern entrance. To the west were the black, wooded humps he knew to be the Bighorn Mountains. Some of the peaks were crested with snow.

Matt belonged out here in the saddle. Frustrated with the politicians and fed up with never getting a straight answer, he preferred being among men like Jasper Mickleson, who could look you straight in the eye.

Matt arrived at Wrangler late in the afternoon, riding in from the north entrance and crossing the wide wooden bridge over the busy creek.

It was a small, quiet town with false fronts on the one saloon to his right and the express office to his left, which advertised the stage and banking. The livery and smithy were behind the express office. Past the saloon, he saw the barbershop, then the town sheriff's office and jail, followed by a small building with a sign reading DISTRICT COURT OFFICE. Past the express office, there was a small two-story hotel followed by two stores. Homes were small and unpretentious. He guessed maybe a hundred people lived in town.

Matt stopped at the barbershop, a

square building with closed fences in the back, probably for bathing. The sign read BARBER, DOCTOR, DENTIST AND UNDERTAKER. Matt went inside and found Tuck, the barber, to be a short man with a thick grey mustache, no hair on his head, and round friendly eyes. There were no customers in the neat shop.

Matt told him about the attack and Bonnie McClain.

'Well, I ain't no real doctor, but if they send for me, I'll see what I can do.'

'You treat any gunshot wounds last night?'

'I'm always treatin' gunshot wounds. There was some shootin' in The Lucky Lady around midnight last night. Two men were shot, but they're all right.'

'Who were they?'

'Listen to me, stranger. You have questions, you talk to the sheriff.'

'I'll do that.'

'But if you need a shave and a bath, I got it.'

'Heat up some water. I'll be back in a half hour.'

Matt was annoyed and left the barber's to go back to the street. He left his roan at the railing in front of the jail and found the boardwalk to be creaky with grass growing up through the cracks. There were only a few men on the street and no sign of women or children.

Entering the jail, he found the town sheriff seated at his desk to the right. Two empty cells were in the back of the single room. On the left was an iron stove, table and chairs. The two large windows in front had sliding wooden shutters on the inside. On each side wall there was a small narrow opening about two inches high and six inches wide, designed as rifle slots.

The town sheriff was a short man with a big belly and protruding eyes, wearing a dirty brown vest and pushing his hat back as he put his hand on his desk to study Matt.

'What do you want, mister?'

'There was trouble out of town about twenty miles northwest of here. Some masked riders forced a wagon off a canyon rim. The McClain family.'

'That so? All killed, were they?'

'McClain died. The woman survived.'

The sheriff frowned. 'Well, now.'

'So are you going out to have a look?'

'What for?'

Matt stood with his thumbs hooked in his gun belt, his skin tight in rising anger. 'To see if you can figure who done it. Before he died, McClain said it was Target riders.'

'He was loco.'

'His wife said one of them was talking French.'

'Lots of men around here from the South. They talk French. McClain had somethin' against young Kerby Driscoll, that's all. Blamed him for all his troubles.'

'I heard he blamed him for his wife's death.'

'Don't know nothin' about that. And if you're smart, you won't ask no questions, neither.'

'What are you goin' to do about McClain's murder?'

'Listen here, stranger, I don't figure I got no say outside this here town. And I don't need you comin' around to tell me how to do my job. So you just get out of here.'

'The doc told me he treated a couple gunshot wounds last night.'

'They were shot in the saloon.'

'Now that's in your jurisdiction. Who were they?'

'Listen, mister, you're tryin' my patience.'

Matt was so angry sweat was dripping down his back. He unhooked his thumbs, his hands dangling at his sides as he glared at the man. Then he turned and started for the door.

'Who are you anyhow?' the sheriff demanded.

'Matt Landry.'

'Hey now, hold on there.'

Matt paused, turning but still grim. 'What for?'

'I didn't know who you was. No, sir. But I know your name, and that's for sure, yes sir. Mr. Driscoll, he allowed as how you was comin' to see him. And I'd be right proud to take you out there.'

'I'll find it.'

'Well now, it's near evenin', so you'll need a room. I'll put in a good word for you at the hotel. And I can get you fixed up at the livery. And if you need any credit at the store, I can arrange it.'

'Don't need any help.'

The sheriff was red-faced, anxious. 'I didn't know who you was, Mr. Landry. You got to know, this is a tough job, and I thought you was some trouble-maker, that's all.'

'So who were the men shot up last night?'

'Well, there was Kid Monet and Sid Crutz. Seems they were drinking too much, and they were trying to do a fast draw and their guns went off, that's all. But they're all right, and they went on home.'

'Was it witnessed?'

'Why sure. The saloon was full of Target riders.'

'And these two, they work for Driscoll?'

'That's right.'

'And how did the first Mrs. McClain die?'

'Well, it was a sorry thing. They found her at the bottom of the canyon. Some man had ravished and beaten her to death. The McClains had hardly been here a month. Weren't nothin' I could do. Why do you want to know?'

Matt shrugged and went outside, shutting the door behind him. Back at the barber's, Matt had a shave inside and a hot bath in the small backyard. The tub sat out back on a wooden platform, and the surrounding fence was over six feet high.

He had put on a clean blue, double-breasted shirt and was just strapping on his Colt when a red-headed man in ranch clothes walked out the back door. He was a short scrawny man in his fifties, his pink face round and clean shaven, his nose flat as if he had been in many fights.

'Hey, you. You got my water dirty.'

Matt frowned. 'I paid for that bath.'

'Well, I'm gonna bury you in it, and you can bet on it.'

3

Matt finished strapping on his Colt. He was standing in front of the deep iron tub of soapy water. The fenced yard was maybe ten-by-fourteen feet. Towels hung on hooks and there was soapy water on the plank platform from Matt's carelessness.

The little man in front of him looked like a little red rooster.

'Draw your own water,' Matt said.

'I paid for this bath.'

'So did I.'

'You're lyin'.'

Matt made a face. 'You call me a liar one more time, I'm goin' to make your nose so flat it'll come out your ears.'

'Maybe you don't know I'm Red Oliver. I've whupped every man in this town. And you can bet on it.'

'That don't scare me none.'

Red rubbed his nose. 'Well, I ain't

wastin' that bath water. You wanna step out front?'

'Nope, I'm all cleaned up, and I got no time for you.'

Pushing his hat back, Red grimaced. 'Here I come!'

Red charged across the six-foot space between them. His pale eyes were round under heavy brows, his mouth twisted in a snarl, his scrawny hands reaching.

Then he slipped on the wet, soapy platform and landed on his rump, sliding wildly toward Matt's legs. Matt lifted one leg, shoved him on through, and kicked him in the rear as he went sailing past. He turned around with a grin.

But then Matt's boots slipped on the soapy water and he fought frantically to keep his balance. He slid and went over backwards, landing on his rear with a loud thump.

Red spun around, still seated on the wet floor.

They glared at each other, and then

the scrawny man began to laugh. ‘You look plumb foolish sittin’ there.’

‘It was your idea.’

‘How about I buy you a drink?’

‘Coffee maybe. I’m plenty hungry.’

‘Got me a room at the hotel. As soon as I have a bath, we’ll have some grub.’

‘Sounds all right. I’ll be puttin’ up my horse.’

They both fought to stand up and slid around. Red lost his balance, his feet went out from under him, and he sat down with a loud splash in the tub, his legs flying up in the air as water went swirling across the floor. He was up to his chin and looking mighty silly.

Matt was grinning. ‘Well, the water’s sure dirty now.’

Red struggled to get back to his feet, one hand on the tub to steady himself.

Matt was grinning. ‘Did you really whup every man in town?’

‘Well, maybe one or two got scared off by my bellerin’. It works, you know. When you’re my size, you gotta try most anything. Who are you anyhow?’

'Matt Landry.'

'Well I'll be. Everyone says you're gonna marry Adriane Driscoll. Me, I got a shirttail outfit. Between McClain's and Target, near the Red Rocks.'

'The old outlaw hangout, I hear.'

'Yeah. And yesterday, I was best man at McClain's weddin'. Even wore me one of them little string ties.'

Matt drew a deep breath, then told him about the attack.

For a long moment Red could only stare at him. Then he spoke with a wavering voice as his eyes misted.

'Had to be Target.'

'There's no proof.'

'Then you get it, Matt Landry.'

Matt wanted to respond in the negative, but the short man's face was so set with trust that Matt could only swallow and turn carefully toward the door, slipping and sliding until he gripped the frame. Water from Red's splash was trailing him.

Matt made it into the carpeted hallway that led to the barbershop, wiping his boots on the thick rug.

'I saw that!' a woman snapped. She had curly red hair and was pudgy with a round pink face. She was maybe five feet high and nearly that round, in her forties, and wearing an apron over a gingham dress. 'You got no manners, mister.'

'You work here?'

'I'm Molly, the owner. My brother Tuck's the barber.' She looked down at the water swirling from the outside onto the rug. 'My heaven. You'll clean that up.'

'Wasn't me. Go see Red Oliver.'

'Red's back there?' she asked, brightening. 'Good thing I'm workin' my day off. He's always avoidin' me.'

'Go get 'im,' Matt said.

She hurried past him, and Matt chuckled, then headed into the barber shop. No wonder it was so clean, he thought. Molly would scrub and polish anything that moved.

In the barber's he paused. A man in his mid-fifties was sitting down in the barber chair. He was thin, greying, and had a furrowed brow, but he was smiling as he spoke to the barber.

'Just a little off the sides, Tuck.'

'You was just in here a few days ago, Judge.'

'Got to keep you busy. We need a barber around here.'

Matt considered him carefully, and then while the justice of the peace got his hair cut, Matt told him about the attack on the McClain wagon and how only Bonnie had survived.

Abnauther frowned. 'County doesn't have enough people to be organized yet, so there's no county sheriff. And Gordon has no authority outside the town limits. Now, I wrote the U.S. Marshal, askin' him to send a deputy. He wrote back, askin' me to swear in a man for him. A bit irregular, but he gave me the authority in writing, and the governor concurred.'

'So when will you have this deputy?'

'Not enough prospects. I had asked Will McClain, and he had turned me down. Hey, Tuck, not so close, eh?'

'You know, Judge, I think you just come in to see Molly,' the barber teased.

Abnauther flushed and got out of the chair, dusting himself off with the white cloth and looking around, but there was no sign of her. He walked outside into the twilight with Matt.

'I didn't catch your name, son.'

'Matt Landry.'

'Oh yes, you and Adriane Driscoll. I heard you studied law with Kingman. You interested in that badge?'

'All I want to do is raise cattle and horses.'

'So the answer's no?'

'That's right, but thanks anyhow.'

Matt wasn't terribly convincing because he had always considered being a lawman like his brothers. He shook the judge's hand and bid him farewell just as Red Oliver came charging out of the shop, his face reddened. Abnauther looked him over, grunted, and walked down the street toward the south end of town.

Matt grinned at Red. 'You and the judge fightin' over Molly?'

'Hey, he can have her. I ain't never gonna get married, you can bet on it. She's a widow and got this idea she oughta marry up with my ranch.'

'You don't look like you had your bath.'

'With Molly around? No, sir. I'm gonna have one back of the hotel. Ain't as good. Water's always cold, but ain't no woman tryin' to help me.'

'Before we go there, I'd like to have a look at the saloon.'

After Matt put up his roan in the livery, the two men walked in the moonlight to the Lucky Lady Saloon. A lantern hung outside the door. A dozen horses were tied up at the railing, and they could hear laughter inside. Smoke curled out the swinging doors. The windows were dirty.

'It'll be mostly Target riders,' Red warned.

Inside the smokey room they found four card tables with men playing poker at two of them. There were several empty tables, and four men were standing at the long bar. Lamps hung on the walls. There was no music, no women, just noisy men with cigarettes and cigars and pipes, arguing over the cards or laughing over a joke. They all looked like cowhands, except the four at the bar.

These four had low slung six-guns, fancy vests, and shirts, and every one of them looked mean as sin.

At the bar a suddenly nervous Red Oliver called to the thin, mustached bartender. 'Whiskey.'

Matt stood next to Red as he looked around the room, then placed two bits on the bar as the bartender poured Red a drink. Matt looked directly at the man behind the bar.

'Heard there was a shootin' here last night.'

'Yep.'

'What happened?'

'Just a little horseplay. What's it to you, mister?'

Matt studied the man. Everyone sure had their story down pat. He looked at the four guns standing near him, and he met the glance of the first one, a man with black eyes, slimy face, thin nose, and draping black mustache.

'You got anything to say?' Matt asked.

The gunman snickered, then poured himself another drink.

'This here's Kid Monet,' the bartender said. 'You'd best be gettin' out of here, mister.'

But one of the men behind Monet came forward. He had a pink face, black beard, and thin mustache. His hat was shoved back from his narrow brow. He had a strong build, and his thick voice was putting on a show for his friends.

'We don't like strangers askin' questions.'

Red started to speak, then fell back at Matt's wave.

'You got a name?' Matt asked.

The man smirked, his hand near his holster. 'Yeah, Sid Crutz. And I figure you oughta just turn and walk right out of here.'

'I'd like a few answers first.'

'This is the only answer you're gonna get.'

The man reached for his gun, but it was only half out of his holster when Matt's Colt leaped into his hand.

There was a hush. Crutz turned pale. He let his six-gun slide back into place. He moistened his lips, staring into the barrel of Matt's Colt. The men at the tables were frozen in place. The bartender backed away.

Kid Monet was still snickering. 'All right, mister, you've had your fun. Now get out of here.'

'The two of you were wounded in here, is that right?'

'Like the man said, horseplay.'

'I understand you speak French.'

'So what? A lot of us do.'

Matt holstered his gun, looking

Monet and Crutz and the other two men over carefully. They were gunmen all right, but Crutz was muscle bound and plenty mad about the gunplay.

'You need to be taught a lesson,' Crutz said, unbuckling his gunbelt.

'I got no fight with you.'

'You hidin' behind that iron, or you got guts?'

Red started to speak, but Matt waved him aside. He wasn't sure he could take Crutz, but he felt a need to establish himself, first with the gun and now with his fists. Maybe then he'd be someone to reckon with, and not just a name connected with the Driscolls. A name they might back away from for reasons Matt didn't like.

Crutz was sneering now, his mouth twisted. 'You are yellow.'

Matt unbuckled his gunbelt and handed it to Red, who backed away to the end of the bar. Crutz waved his arms, and the other men made room.

Matt stood with his hands at his side, waiting. He knew Crutz had been embarrassed by the gunplay and was determined to beat Matt to a pulp, anything to regain his reputation.

But Matt had an edge. He believed this man was one of the killers back on the ridge, and fury was driving him with renewed strength.

'Let's see what you got,' Crutz said, dancing about, hands outstretched like a bare-knuckle fighter.

Matt shot his fist in, struck Crutz on the jaw, and darted aside. Crutz's head snapped back, and he was dazed, eyes blazing like black marbles.

'You better stand still, mister.'

But Matt darted in from the side, clobbered Crutz on the jaw, and darted away again. Furious, Crutz charged. Matt went to jump aside and was tripped by one of the onlookers. He staggered, and Crutz plowed into his middle.

The two men grappled, fighting to stay upright, yet pounding each other's bellies right and left. Matt ducked and slammed his head against Crutz's jaw.

It made both men dizzy, and they broke apart.

Both were sweating, but Crutz was beginning to realize he was not going to win so easily. He turned and grabbed a wooden chair, raising it and shoving it at Matt's face. Matt ducked as Crutz charged and kicked him in the rear.

Roaring with anger, Crutz spun around, chair in hand. Matt slammed his fist in Crutz's middle. Eyes wild, Crutz doubled up, gasping for air and dropping the chair. Matt's fist landed on the man's chin, snapping his head back. Crutz staggered backwards, holding his middle as Matt hit him on the jaw once more. Crutz sank to his knees, eyes rolling. He fell forward and lay still.

Matt straightened, gasping for air, sweat drenching him.

Kid Monet was leaning on the bar, smiling with amusement. The others were just staring. Matt calmly took his gun belt from Red and buckled it on very slowly.

'This is only round one,' Monet said. 'You'll be dead by the end of the week.'

Matt backed toward the swinging doors, and a nervous Red backed with him. Red couldn't resist pausing to hit them hard with his words.

'Maybe you fellas don't know it, but this here's Matt Landry.'

Monet's lips curved down at one corner.

Matt and Red backed out of the smokey room and headed into the cold night air. 'Them four weren't cow-hands,' Matt said.

Red was wiping his brow. 'Well, you made 'em mad all right, but I made 'em madder. They can't go after you because you're gonna marry Driscoll's daughter. But what I wanna know is, why'd you go after them in the first place?'

'I didn't want to be known as her fiancé.'

'Well, they sure know who you are now. But they're a mighty dangerous lot. Saloon belongs to a fellow name

Fowler. Used to be a tradin' post, and word is he took good care of Pollard and his friends.'

'They could have been behind the McClain killin'.'

'Maybe, but you ain't never gonna find out nothin',' Red said. 'Besides, I heard you turn down the judge when he offered you a badge. So if you ain't gonna be a lawman, and all you wanna do is marry Adriane Driscoll, how come you're so curious about the shootin'?'

'I keep thinkin' about Will McClain.'

'Yeah, and that poor woman from Missouri.'

They crossed the street to the small hotel, which was full, so Matt was grateful when Red offered to share his room. They each enjoyed a big beefsteak and good hot coffee in the hotel cafe.

Matt looked around at the empty tables. There were a lot of plates stacked up on one of them, so it had been busy. But right now it was near silent. Except for Red's monologue.

Leaning back, Matt sipped his coffee. 'Tell me about the first Mrs. McClain.'

'Some man killed her all right.'

'Any ideas?'

Red hesitated, making sure the waiter was out of earshot. 'Well, a lot of men admired her. But Kerby Driscoll, he figured she ought to jump right in his arms. Everyone laughed at him, but —'

'Why would he do it?'

'I don't know, Matt. Maybe he didn't.'

After a long night in the hotel with Red snoring so much that Matt had to move his bunk to the far wall, Matt awakened early. As Red lay sputtering in his sleep across the room Matt stared at the dark ceiling and the moonlight through the dirty curtains on the window.

He was thinking of Adriane. He had been getting weary of politics about the time he met her, but she was so swept up in Governor Hoyt's pride in Matt that he couldn't do anything but agree he would try to be governor someday. He knew it had impressed her, and he had fallen all over himself pleasing her. But now she might well be angry at his decision to be a rancher instead.

When Red awakened, they pulled on their boots. The little man offered to guide him most of the way to Target.

'My place is between McClain's and Target. Got me a couple hundred head and two hands. McClain, he got three hands and maybe three hundred head.'

'Good start.'

'But when the land opened up, Target brought in twenty-five thousand head of Texas cattle right off and filled up the grass all the way to the Powder River, with maybe forty hands. But they're bringin' more cattle and men, and they want us out. Once they get me and McClain's, they'll roll on over the rest of 'em.'

'So you agree that was no accident in the canyon.'

'If you mean do I think they was just harrassin' the newlyweds? Well, I figure they was plannin' to run 'em off all the time. They just was bein' mean about it.'

At breakfast in the hotel cafe there were several merchants and two cow-hands, but Red and Matt found an empty table. They had steak and beans, and Matt had trouble concentrating on his food. All he could think about was Adriane and what was being said about the two of them.

It was then the waiter came with fresh coffee and paused to stare past them. The three men turned in their chairs to follow the old man's gaze.

Standing in the doorway was Jasper Mickleson, blood on his shirt.

4

Matt stood up quickly from the breakfast table. Red Oliver leaned back in his chair, staring at the bleeding Jasper, who was staggering forward with Tuck holding his arm.

'Gordon won't do nothin'. I went to the judge and he can't do nothin', but he sent me over here.'

'Abnauther sent you here?' Matt asked.

'Yeah, he said you was the only one who'd do something.'

Matt moved forward to grab the cowhand's other arm and lead him to a chair. Blood was trickling down from the side of Jasper's head where he had obviously been clubbed. He was dazed as he sat down.

Tuck had a wet towel and was dabbing at the wounds.

'What happened?' Matt asked.

'Me and Todd, we was lookin' for strays. We got ambushed. They shot Todd right out of the saddle. I tried to pull my six shooter, but a bullet creased me, and I was thrown into the rocks. Guess they thought I was dead. When I come to, they was gone.'

'You recognize any of 'em?'

'Didn't even see 'em. And Todd's dead,' he added grimly.

'Where's Single-Foot?'

'He'd gone elk hunting and won't be back to the ranch yet. Will you help us, Matt?'

For a long moment Matt thought of Todd, the young, fresh-faced cowhand he had met briefly. Then he thought of Adriane, who had come into his life and overwhelmed him. She was waiting for him.

So why was he still here, having breakfast and considering helping Jasper find Todd's killers? And why was he so worried about Bonnie McClain?

'It ain't fair,' Red Oliver said. 'Matt's gettin' married. You got no right to put this on him.'

Jasper was grim as he scratched at the dry blood on his shirt. 'Well, I reckon you're right. And that means nobody's gonna stop 'em. They're gonna kill anybody they want.'

Red rubbed his nose. 'This proves Will McClain's death was no accident.'

'As long as there ain't no law here,' Jasper mumbled, 'ain't nothin' goin' to stop 'em.'

'What about the army?' Matt asked.

'Fort McKinney's too far away, too small, and got its hands full with stray bands of Sioux what been raidin' south of it. And I hear they're gonna move the fort anyhow.'

After a long deep thought Matt shrugged. 'I could ride along with you to the McClain ranch and then go to the Driscolls from there.'

'I'd sure appreciate it,' Jasper said, relieved. 'Now I gotta go get patched up.'

'Can you make it by yourself?'

'Yeah. I've hurt worse ridin' broncs.'

Matt watched the weary cowhand get up and walk unsteadily out the door. He turned to the amused Red Oliver who was chuckling.

'Yeah, what's the matter with you?'

'I got you figured out, Matt Landry. You ain't one bit anxious to get hitched. You got cold feet. That's what you got, and you can bet on it.'

'I'm just doin' the man a favor.'

'What do you bet you ride out of town with a badge?'

'Not a chance.'

Again Matt reflected. Adriane would have a hard time with a badge. He had committed himself to her but was having too many misgivings about the marriage to back off on his ranching dreams. To go a step further with a badge, well, he didn't figure that was fair.

'Matt Landry,' a voice called.

They turned to see Abnauther standing in the doorway. The judge looked grim and determined, and Matt stood up as Abnauther came to join them. They all sat down, and the judge ordered a cup of coffee.

'Jasper tells me you're ridin' out with him.'

'Just doin' a favor.'

'Well, you get out there and have a look, that's fine. But what if you find the tracks and decide to follow 'em? What then?'

Matt shrugged. 'I ain't plannin' no fight.'

'Yes, well, you would be outnumbered. You and an old cowhand and that Apache scout. Just the three of you against a dozen killers. You would be a fool to try it.'

'Okay, Judge, spit it out.'

'Seems to me you'd be a lot better off to be wearin' a badge when you go gettin' into trouble.'

'I'm not takin' your badge.'

'How about one day's worth?'

Matt made a face. 'You're tryin' to trick me.'

'No, I just think you could take the badge. I'd swear you in, and then you could turn it back in tomorrow.'

'Why do I need it in the first place?'

'Because when you and Jasper and Single-Foot start trackin', you want to have some kinda control, don't you?'

'I'm wearin' the control, right here on my hip.'

'That won't scare them none.'

'And a badge will?'

'Might slow 'em down.'

'My brothers are all lawmen, and not once did they ever tell me a badge scared anyone. It just makes 'em targets.'

'Why are we arguing?' Abnauther asked. 'You know blamed well you're going to take the badge.'

Matt drew a deep breath as the judge held out his hand. The gleaming star read DEPUTY U.S. MARSHAL. It was silver and encircled with a shining rim. As Matt stared at it, he knew he wanted that star on his vest.

Abnauther bounced the silver in his hand. 'As soon as I got the authority I had the smithy make it out of Mexican silver dollars.'

Matt swallowed hard, his throat bitter dry. As the brother who had had the opportunity to study law, Matt's natural inclination to be on his horse had been curtailed. But he had always wanted more action than he had found among the politicians. And here was action gleaming silver. He couldn't resist, and he found himself nodding.

'Just 'til I get back to town.'

Abnauther smiled. 'Stand up, Matt Landry, and hold up your right hand.'

Matt obeyed.

'Repeat after me. I solemnly swear to uphold the laws of this territory and the constitution of these United States. So help me God.'

Matt repeated the words. ' . . . so help me God.'

Abnauther's wiry hands pinned the circled star on Matt's leather vest, and Matt felt a warm glow that seemed to swell in him. Looking down at the gleaming silver with short breath and perspiration on his brow, he struggled to appear nonchalant.

'You'll get it back.'

'Be sure to swear in anybody who rides with you.'

Abnauther grinned and backed away. He clasped his hands together, his pale eyes twinkling, then walked out of the cafe.

Matt sat down, polishing the star with his bandanna. Then he noticed the merchants and two cowhands staring at him. Abruptly, the two hands got up and left the cafe.

Red Oliver sipped his coffee. 'Well, there goes two Target men. And they sure enough are headin' back to the ranch to spread the word.'

Matt shrugged, almost grateful the news would get to Adriane before he would have to tell her.

'But don't worry,' Red added. 'If Adriane Driscoll is the woman you think she is, she'll go right along with you.'

'Are you ridin' with us? You got a ranch out there. And you have men workin' for you, don't you? What makes you think you're safe? Somebody's out to terrorize the McClains, and you could be next.'

Red shrugged. 'So you and me and Jasper, and Single-Foot. Four of us against a dozen or more.'

'Got anyone else?'

'Some other ranchers, but they're scattered way out. Ain't no one in this town brave enough to go out there. All sittin' here nice and safe and kissin' Driscoll's feet. But if you think a scrawny coot like me can do anything, I'll go.'

Matt grinned. 'I suspect you can hold your own.'

They went outside into the morning sunlight. Matt told himself it was reasonable to put on this badge and head out after killers. No one else was going to do it. And he had liked young Todd, and maybe he was worried about Bonnie. He told himself Adriane would understand and be proud of him.

* * *

At the Target ranch, Adriane was standing in the parlor with her father and brother as an excited young cowhand told them about the judge and the badge. Adriane, wearing a new green silk dress with velvet trim, her hair done up in large curls, was aghast. 'You must be wrong.'

'No, Ma'am. He told the judge he would give that there badge back to him when the hunt was over.'

The cowhand left the house, and Adriane was furious, pacing about and waving her fan. 'How could he do this to me? Why isn't he rushing here to be with me?'

Kerby Driscoll, running his hand through his fluffy, light brown hair, was wearing a new plaid shirt of soft wool. He fingered his low-slung Colt, then stretched and smiled as he pulled on his Stetson. There was a small scar on his forehead. He had his father's wide nose and hard jaw, but he was good-looking in an odd sort of way. He sat down and crossed one leg over the other. He was pleased to see his sister upset. 'Now, Adriane, every man can't crawl at your feet.'

'He was wild about me. He should be here right now.'

King Driscoll's heavy brows lifted as he sat in his fancy chair. 'Adriane, will you please sit down?'

'But your future son-in-law is wearing a badge.'

'Just for the hunt.'

'And what if he doesn't take it off?'

'Then we'll have a lawman on our side, and you can handle him, can't you?'

'I'm not so sure.'

Kerby yawned. 'Well, I'm goin' back to town.'

'Young man,' King said, 'I'm getting tired of you disappearing all the time.'

'Every time I play poker, I come out a winner.'

'Well, this time I want you to stay here.'

Kerby stood up, adjusting his gun belt, his face darkening as he sobered. He was a man of average height, but he came across as fearless and powerful.

'Sorry, Pa. I have business to take care of.'

'And what about the ranch? The only way we can have this valley all to ourselves is to work at it. That doesn't mean playing poker.'

'You know I never was much of a hand with cows. You neither, Pa. We're in this for the money, remember? And I pass on your orders, don't I? Besides, there's more than one way to get a ranch.'

'What's that supposed to mean?'

Kerby smiled. 'Bonnie McClain.'

'She's still alive, but she's grieving. And you get to drinking, you may say something you shouldn't. So you stay away from her,' King warned.

'I want to have a look at her. McClain's first wife was really somethin', so I figure —'

'Kerby, haven't you learned anything yet?'

Kerby's face was strained, and Adriane quickly changed the subject. 'You know, Kerby, you shouldn't be seen with those outlaws.'

'Monet? He's a real gunfighter. I can learn from him.'

King frowned. 'Just be sure he learns nothing from you.'

Kerby just smiled and quickly left the parlor, but Adriane was not interested in her brother's problems. All she wanted to know was why Matt wasn't racing to her side. She was so angry, she broke her fan.

* * *

While she was steaming, Matt felt his ears burning.

As he rode in the cold wind with Red and Jasper, their horses trudging through the muddy ground, he wondered if Adriane was angry with him. Maybe that's why his face was so hot.

He parted his heavy coat and looked down at the silver badge on his vest. It seemed to belong there. He had felt natural when he had sworn Red and Jasper in as his deputies; as if he had done it for years.

They paused to rest in a gully, watching a buzzard circling in the distance. Red leaned on his pommel, studying Matt. 'What makes a man wanna pin one of them stars on himself?'

Matt shrugged. 'I ain't sure. Maybe we see ourselves as bein' noble. We think we can make a difference.'

'Out here?'

Matt had to silently agree with Red. The only difference he was likely to make was another grave. They left the gully and headed on into the wind.

At the end of the day Jasper shifted his weight in the saddle. 'Well, we covered a lot of ground and lost the tracks. It'll be dark soon. Now we got to get Single-Foot. If there are any signs, he'll find 'em.'

At the small McClain ranch they saw a skinned elk wrapped in gunny sacks hanging high on the limb of a cottonwood near a small creek. It had a limb through the hocks and had already shed its antlers. It was plenty big and would feed the ranch for some time.

The house was nestled within the rolling hills and scattered pines. It was small and square with a big chimney in back of the board roof and had a lean-to giving shelter to firewood. Nearby was a series of shacks and several corrals. Four horses stood inside the fence with their backs to the cold wind.

On a far slope a dozen head of cattle grazed.

Single-Foot was coming out of one of the shacks that apparently served as a bunkhouse, and he paused to watch them ride up. The door to the house opened, and Bonnie McClain, wearing an old wool coat and carrying a bucket, came outside.

The icy breeze was tossing her yellow hair.

Matt reined up and stared at her a long moment.

Jasper turned in the saddle. 'Well, Matt, I already told her you was marryin' that Driscoll woman.'

'And?'

'She ain't thinkin' too kindly of you.'

Single-Foot stood quietly as the three men dismounted. Red Oliver tipped his hat several times to Bonnie. Matt touched his hat brim, and Jasper removed his hat as she approached.

'Jasper, I'm glad you're back. And Mr. Oliver.'

Matt's face was burning. She was ignoring him, her chin in the air as she greeted the others.

'Mrs. McClain,' Jasper said, 'would you sit over there on that bench for a moment?'

She paled and obeyed. 'What is it, Jasper?'

'Todd and me, yesterday we was out huntin' strays and got ambushed. Todd was shot right off, and they left me for dead. I buried him out there.'

Tears filled her eyes. 'Oh, not Todd.'

'We been huntin' 'em,' Red told her. 'We found their tracks, then lost 'em. We figure they was headed for the Red Rock canyons back of my place. But my boys didn't see nothin'.'

Single-Foot's face was dark and grim. 'I will find them.'

'No,' she said, anxious. 'They'll be waiting for you.'

'Matt here was helping us,' Jasper added.

She stood up with color hot in her cheeks. 'What for, Matt Landry? Why aren't you out at Target kissing King Driscoll's feet? After all, you're going to marry all those cattle.'

Matt's coat parted as he stiffened, and she saw the silver badge gleaming in the last rays of the sun. She stared at the badge as she wiped at her tears.

'We got us a new deputy marshal,' Jasper told her.

Red grunted. 'The judge talked him

into it. Just for this posse, that is.'

Matt swallowed hard, a trickle of sweat down his back.

'It makes a good show,' she said crisply. 'Well, all of you may as well come up to the house for some elk, seeing as how Single-Foot went through a lot of trouble to get it.'

As night fell around them they headed up the hill and into the small house for supper. The stone fireplace had cooking pots hanging over the burning logs. A large stack of wood was to the left, and there was a table and six chairs. To the right there was a tattered couch and a back room.

Bonnie busied herself at the stove, her voice still icy. 'I hear the Driscolls have rosewood furniture.'

'You'll have it someday,' Jasper promised.

'Well, I'm just wondering if the new deputy is too proud to sit on those old chairs.'

Matt frowned, but she had just lost her husband, and he wasn't about to fight with her. Her irritation with him continued through the delicious supper.

Matt fingered his coffee cup and turned to the Apache, who had stuffed himself. 'Single-Foot, have you been up in those Red Rocks?'

'One time.'

Jasper nodded. 'It's mighty hostile country, and there's a lot of sandstone. Those fellas could be hiding anyplace.'

'Or they could have gone back to Target,' Red commented.

'Either way,' Matt said, 'we've got to find 'em.'

Red grunted. 'If they don't find us first.'

5

It was decided that Jasper should stay on the ranch to protect Bonnie, especially since he was not over his headaches and was having some double vision.

Matt was still smarting from her cold anger.

After combing the Red Rocks for two days, Matt, Red, and Single-Foot found no signs of the masked riders. Matt used his spyglass constantly but to no avail. Single-Foot scanned the earth in vain for anything, a rock out of its dirt socket, a bent strand of grass.

It was raining again as they headed back to Red's place. They spent the night in the old house that had once served as a hideout. There were rifle slots in the walls and wooden shutters over the windows.

Out back, there was a stable for

twenty horses near the corrals. Red's two hands were in a shack that also served as a tack room. One of them, Stoney, was always grinning. The other, Chip, was grouchy and getting on in years.

Red had an iron stove and plenty of wood stacked up inside. His home was dirty and disheveled, and Matt couldn't help but comment.

'Maybe you and Molly ought to get together. She'd clean up this place.'

'Don't even think it,' Red responded with a grunt. 'But the match I'd like to make is Stoney and Driscoll's house-maid. Both about the same age. Stoney ain't met her, but he figures she'd be too high-toned. He loves bein' a cowhand, you know. Best man I ever saw with a horse.'

'Why did Big-Nose Pollard pull out of this hide-out?'

'Best I can figure is when the Target herds come rollin' in, he reckoned as how he'd make more money with Driscoll.'

Single-Foot, who was silent, stared into his coffee cup.

Matt turned to the Apache. 'You did your best.'

'We find 'em,' Single-Foot said, 'at Target.'

'I'll go on there alone,' Matt said. 'If they are Driscoll riders, maybe I can smoke 'em out.'

Red downed his coffee. 'So the hunt is over. What about that badge?'

Matt had grown fond of the silver. 'Well, maybe I'll show it to Miss Driscoll. See what she says.'

'She won't like it,' Red told him. 'But if you take it off to please her, she'll have you under her thumb for good. So you'd better make up your mind afore you get there. You got an all-day ride, so do your figurin' in the saddle.'

Matt couldn't sleep that night. He kept thinking of Bonnie moving around the stove and kitchen table. That was the way he had first thought of Adriane. He tossed and turned.

The next day, Matt headed east

toward the distant black butte behind the Driscoll ranch house. He rode for hours, and as late afternoon came he realized he was dirty and unkempt. He stopped at a creek to wash his face, but it was too icy-cold to bathe. He rode onward, figuring Adriane would be so happy to see him that she would not care.

He neared a grazing herd of some forty steers, then he saw more on the far rolling hills. Soon he realized there were thousands spotting the distant landscape. Target Cattle Company or not, Driscoll was overgrazed and would need a lot more grass.

Toward evening four riders came to meet him, and Matt covered his badge with his coat. They came to a halt, blocking his path. They were young and fearless, but when he gave his name they hurriedly escorted him to the ranch.

It was nearly dark when they arrived at the elaborate spread. Corrals were strong and well kept and filled with horses. There was a large, solid barn and a bunk-house with a lot of sheds. Everything was neat and in good repair.

The house was enormous and set on a knoll. It had two stories with a veranda upstairs and a porch circling the first floor. Near the front door was a porch swing.

Matt swallowed, his throat dry, lips parched. He knew he smelled of sweat and was dirty. When Adriane saw how he looked and that he was wearing a badge, she might well be angry, he reconsidered.

The men took care of his horse, and he stood in front of the big walnut door, afraid to knock. Finally, he pounded.

The door was opened after a few minutes by a small woman in her twenties. She gazed up at him with wide eyes.

'Matt Landry,' he said.

She smiled and backed away, letting him enter. He kept his coat and held his hat in his hands. She led him to the parlor and bid him to wait.

He was alone, admiring the fine paintings and plush furnishings. He felt he was back in Cheyenne, getting ready to go to McDaniel's Variety Theater or a meeting with the stockgrowers.

'Matt!'

He turned to see Adriane hurrying toward him. She looked lovely in a blue dress with lace at the collar. He remembered now what had drawn him to her: that sweet smile, that charm, that gracious manner, the excitement and beauty of her. And yet as he gazed at her, he realized she was still a stranger.

She came right up to him and took his arm. Standing on her tiptoes, she kissed him square on the mouth. She smelled of lilac, but she drew back, sniffing.

'Oh, Matt, you're filthy. Where have you been?'

'There's a band of killers out there. We were hunting them.'

'Yes, I heard.'

'They murdered Will McClain and one of his hands. Somebody had to do something.'

She pouted. 'But it didn't have to be you, Matt. I've been waiting and waiting. And when I heard you put on a badge, oh, Matt, I was very upset.'

He swallowed. 'It's temporary.'

She reached over and parted his coat, staring at the silver. 'The hunt is over, so take it off.'

'The killers are still out there, and whatever they're plannin', it ain't over.'

'Matt, what about our plans? I don't want Father to meet you like this. Come, I'll have Lenny draw you a bath.'

As he bathed in the papered room with velvet trim all around Matt stared into space. He wondered now if he had only been infatuated with Adriane. Yet he was committed. A man's word had to mean something, but he felt as if a chain was hanging around his neck.

Maybe the badge would delay things, give him a chance to think it out, to come to grips with what he really felt.

It was later when he was cleaned up that Matt returned to the parlor to find Adriane and her father waiting. King Driscoll was cordial with a strong handshake, and he invited Matt to have supper with them.

When they had eaten and were having their coffee in front of the stone hearth with a blazing fire, Matt could feel the rancher's distrust. Adriane sat next to Matt on the couch, her hand on his arm. 'What do you think of our home, Matt?'

'Sure didn't expect it out here.'

'We can't live the way the rest of these people do. Now listen, Matt, we're going to have a big party and announce our betrothal.'

'You're going to marry a lawman?' her father asked.

'Oh, gracious no. Matt's going to turn in that badge when he gets back to town, aren't you, Matt?'

Matt shrugged. 'I ain't so sure when. I've got to see this thing through. Good men are dead, and no one is doing anything about it.'

'But, Matt,' she pleaded. 'You came here to marry me, and we were going to live in Cheyenne, remember?'

Her father stood up slowly. 'I'm going to retire. You two can work it out. But let me tell you this, Matt, I wouldn't be too happy having my daughter married to a lawman. She'd be a widow too soon.'

'Wait, Mr. Driscoll. There's something I got to say.'

'Yes?'

'Mrs. McClain said that when the riders attacked their wagon, her husband said they were your men.'

'Target men?'

'He said they were Target riders.'

'He saw their faces?'

'No, their faces were covered with bandannas.'

'So there you have it. He was obviously mistaken.'

'Some of your men are hired guns. Like Monet and Crutz.'

'Matt, how can you question my

father like this?'

'It's all right, honey. He has to ask. So I'll tell you, Matt. Some of my men are hard cases, yes, but rustlers are rampant along the Powder River. They're bound to spread out this way. I need men who can handle themselves.'

Matt shrugged, and when her father was out of the room Adriane sat up straight at his side.

'Matt, you're acting so strange.'

'We have to talk, Adriane.'

She was wary, annoyed. 'What is it now?'

'Back in Cheyenne, I kind of led you to believe I wanted to stay in politics. But once I got on the trail and away from all that, I had a chance to remember how it was when I was a lot happier. And I got to figurin', all I want to do is raise cattle and horses. So once this job is done, I — '

'Matt, you can't be serious.'

'I was a cowhand before I ever studied law.'

'This doesn't sound like you at all.'

'What's wrong with a ranch and a bunch of kids? I've saved enough to get us started. I'm not plannin' to live off your father.'

'Matt, it's out of the question.'

'What do you mean?'

'We have everything working for you. All those men are behind you back in Cheyenne. They won't let you quit, Matt.'

'They'll forget about me.'

She drew a deep breath in anger, then looked away as if she was gathering her thoughts. After a long moment she turned slowly, a sweet smile on her face. The same smile he remembered from Cheyenne, one that came so easily to her. But her eyes were darkened.

'All right, Matt. A rancher if you wish. But no badge.'

'When they catch the killers, the badge comes off.'

'But what if you never find them?'

'If the trail runs cold, I'll turn it in.'

'Promise?'

He nodded reluctantly. Nothing seemed right anymore.

But when she put her hand to his face and kissed him warmly, he tried to remember how it had been, tried to relive the excitement. He put his hand on her soft curls and kissed her back, and felt as if he had only kissed her portrait.

'Now then, Matt, you need a good-night's sleep.'

But Matt didn't sleep that night, tossing and turning on the feather bed. At breakfast on the veranda King sat between them as Adriane told him of Matt's decision.

'You know, Matt,' King said, 'I was your age once and going in all directions. Someday, you'll end up where you belong, and I believe you'll find it will be where you can do the most good. That's why I'm here now. And that's why you'll be back in politics afore long.'

Matt shrugged. 'Adriane told me you had a ranch in Ohio.'

'Well, I was a gentleman rancher. Had all the money. Sat on the porch and gave orders.'

'You like it better out here?'

'A man likes power, Matt. You'll find that out someday. But we'll hear no more about you getting your own ranch. If that's the life you want, you'll share in Target with Adriane.'

Adriane was anxious, gripping her fan very tight.

* * *

Matt left early that morning, Adriane's kiss warm on his lips. He should have headed straight for town, but he wandered the hills, seeing the herds Adriane's father had promised he would share. There was a lot of wealth about to be bestowed upon him, and he felt odd about it. And about her.

He spent the night in the hills, far from the Target herd. He needed to be alone, to gather his thoughts, to hear the coyotes' howls in the distance.

Sadness came over him as he rolled in his blankets.

As he slept with the fire smouldering he heard a sound, and his hand rested on his six-gun under his blankets. Tense, sweat on his back, he turned his gaze toward the fire. There, sniffing its way through his possibles, was the black dog.

Matt sat up slowly. 'So you're back.'

The dog jumped, hardtack in its teeth.

Grinning, Matt lay back in his blankets, watching the dog make itself at home near the fire. He hoped it would stay. The dog no longer snarled. In fact, its tail flopped.

'Why are you takin' up with a lawman?'

Again the tail flopped, and Matt was right happy when the dog came over to lie at his side.

'Maybe there'll come a time when you'll stick with me, and I'd be right glad if you did.'

Matt was in no hurry and spent

another night on the trail, mostly because the dog was there, and he needed some quiet time with company that didn't talk. In fact, it was so peaceful, Matt felt a kinship with the dog. They both had been on a long rein, and now they could lie here under the stars together.

On the way to town Matt was pleased that the dog was ahead of him on the trail. When they arrived late morning, the judge was standing outside of his office. Matt reined up and dismounted, draping his reins over the railing.

Abnauther had his arms folded and was leaning on a post, his face set in a scowl. 'No luck?'

'We even went into the Red Rocks. Nothing.'

'I heard you outdrew Sid Crutz and whupped him besides. He's not going to forget about it. As long as you're going to marry Miss Driscoll, they'll leave you be. But you'd better watch your back just the same. Crutz holds a grudge, and if he can get away with an ambush, he might just go ahead.'

Matt shoved his hat back from his damp brow, and his grey-blue eyes squinted in the sunlight. 'Buy you a cup of coffee?'

The judge nodded, and they crossed over to the cafe in the hotel. Blackie followed and lay down on the boardwalk outside. The cafe was empty. The elderly waiter brought them thick, hot coffee, and Matt leaned back in his chair, feeling weary.

'Things are gettin' complicated. I promised Adriane that sooner or later I would turn in my badge.'

'But what's your next move?'

Matt sipped his coffee and studied it. 'I ain't sure what I can do. Trail's runnin' cold.'

'Maybe you'll get lucky. But watch out for Kid Monet and his friends. They're a bad lot.'

'What about the sheriff?'

'Gordon is having a fit, all right. But right now, I figure your job is to stop Target from rolling over the small ranchers. Driscoll and his European backers are going to make a lot of money out of this, and he needs more grass. I've been told he's got more cattle moving north.'

'You got to know, I'm still marrying Miss Driscoll.'

'Don't matter, Matt. You're a born lawman. You'll do what has to be done. I'll give you a map of the ranches so you can call on all of them.'

At that moment Sheriff Gordon appeared in the doorway, his shirt split open over his big belly. He glared at Matt and the shining badge, and he hooked his thumbs in his gun belt with a snarl.

'What you're doin', Judge, it ain't legal.'

'I say it is. Join us for coffee?'

'I ain't sittin' with Landry.'

'You changed your tune,' Matt said. 'The other day, you couldn't be friendly enough.'

'Well, you look like a turncoat to me. And if I was King Driscoll, I wouldn't trust you, and I'm gonna tell 'im so.'

Before Matt could answer, they heard shots ring out.

'At the saloon!' the waiter said from the window.

6

Sheriff Gordon grunted and left the cafe with Abnauther and Matt on his heels, the dog following. They crossed the street and walked up to the saloon where several men were peering through the swinging doors.

'All right, break it up,' Gordon snapped.

Entering the saloon, they found a man dead at a poker table, lying back in his chair and staring at the ceiling, six-gun on the floor. Four other hands were sitting at a far table. Kid Monet and his men, including Crutz, were at the bar. The bartender and a swarthy man were behind the bar.

Facing the dead body was a man with a hard jaw and wide nose, light brown hair, and a fancy wool shirt, six-shooter in hand. He was snickering.

Gordon made a face. 'Well, Kerby, what now?'

'He drew on me, Sheriff.'

'That's right,' said Monet.

The other men and the bartender nodded in agreement.

'Well, you shot 'im. Get rid of 'im,' the sheriff said.

Kerby smiled, slowly holstering his weapon. 'You should have seen it, Sheriff. He drew first, and I still got 'im.'

'It was a fair fight,' the bartender said.

The other man behind the bar came forward. He was dressed like a dandy with fancy vest and gold watch chain, a smirk on his thin face. 'My boys will take care of the body.'

Abnauther cleared his throat. 'Matt Landry, this here's Mr. Fowler. He owns this place.'

Fowler extended his hand, but Matt didn't take it.

'And that's Kerby Driscoll.'

Kerby pushed his hat back. 'Well

now, you sure do get around, Mr. Landry.'

Matt could hear snickers from Monet and his men, and he saw the devilment in Kerby's pale brown eyes. Abnauther shook his head and went to the door, but Matt paused to look from Kerby to Fowler.

'Things are going to change around here,' Matt said.

Gordon stiffened. 'You got no jurisdiction in my town.'

'It's not a town,' Abnauther corrected. 'It's a group of buildings with a mayor. And your jurisdiction is at the pleasure of the people who live here.'

The sheriff sneered, hooking his thumbs in his gun belt.

Fowler smiled lazily and leaned back on the bar. 'Come around any time, Marshal. Free drinks.'

Matt was grim, but he went outside with Abnauther.

They both turned to watch a wagon heading into town. It was Bonnie and Jasper. She looked wonderful in an old leather coat over her gingham dress, her yellow hair blowing in the wind.

He heard Kerby behind him. 'Well, look at her.'

Jasper nodded as they passed, and Bonnie looked coldly at Matt. Kerby came charging out and hurried to the wagon, walking alongside of it and removing his hat.

'Mrs. McClain, I'm Kerby Driscoll. I sure am sorry about your husband. Now if there's anything I can do, you name it.'

The wagon continued onward, and Kerby stopped with a sweep of his hat. Her chilling glance didn't faze him. When he turned, he was grinning happily.

Kerby walked past the annoyed Matt and Abnauther and went into the saloon as the body was dragged out the back door. 'Wow! What a woman. You didn't tell me she was gorgeous, Monet. I figure I'm gettin' hitched.'

Monet snickered. 'I never saw her face before. And you're not the only man in town's going to be after her.'

'She gets to know me, she ain't never gonna pay you no mind. Leave her alone.'

'So no ridin' on the McClain ranch?'

'I didn't say that. Just don't lay a hand on her, got that?'

Fowler poured them all a drink. 'You know, Kerby, you're never satisfied. You wanted McClain's first wife, and now you want his second. Aren't you being a bit greedy?'

Kerby downed his drink. 'She's mine, so hands off.'

'What about Landry?' Monet asked.

'I don't care about him.'

'So you wouldn't mind if I cut him down?'

Kerby smiled, smacking his lips. 'Think you're fast enough?'

'I'm faster than anybody.'

* * *

Away from the saloon and down the street, Bonnie was at the store with

Jasper. She was smiling at the judge and being cold to Matt. The dog was lying near the doorway, head on its paws, eyes following Matt's every move. As Jasper gave the order to the storekeeper she stood on the boardwalk, the wind softly blowing her hair.

'You know, Judge, this is really wonderful country. It's so big. And it's beautiful everywhere you look.'

'So you don't miss Missouri?' Abnauther asked.

'No, not anymore.' She knelt in front of the dog, which lifted its head, watching her carefully. 'So, you took up with a lawman. Well, you behave yourself.'

'I reckon you just met Kerby Driscoll,' Matt said as the judge walked away. He was alone with her as she stood up slowly and turned to face him. She looked aloof, annoyed to be alone with him.

'Yes, but Red told me you couldn't find any of the killers, and that there's no evidence it was the Driscolls.'

'That's right.'

'Maybe I can get proof from Kerby.'

'You stay away from him. He's dangerous. In fact, he just killed a man in the saloon as easy as swattin' a fly.'

She leaned on a post under the roof overhang, her blue-green eyes fixed on him. 'So how is Miss Driscoll?'

'All right.'

'I'm sure they're delighted they'll soon have the law in their family.'

Matt grimaced, anger rising. 'You could be wrong about them, and your husband could have been wrong about the riders.'

She stiffened. 'Oh? And who else would have a reason to kill him? The Driscolls are the only ones who had anything to gain. You're blind, Matt.'

He came to stand a little closer, but she turned away.

It was then she stiffened, for Kerby Driscoll was hurrying down the board-walk toward them, his hand under his hat to smooth his hair. Annoyed, Matt watched as Kerby bowed to her. Her aloofness only made Kerby more ardent.

'You'll love me when you get to know me, Mrs. McClain.'

Jasper came out with a sack of flour and paused, also annoyed. Bonnie was trying to be a lady, while Matt fumed.

'My sister's givin' a dance one day soon,' Kerby said. 'For her and Matt Landry here. Please come.'

Bonnie was uneasy. 'I don't think I'll be going.'

Kerby stepped closer. 'It'll give us a chance to get acquainted.'

She considered this. 'I'll let you know.'

When Kerby had finally strutted away, Bonnie put her hand on the post to steady herself.

'Women must be scarce out here,' she said.

Jasper grunted as he continued to load the wagon, Matt helping him. Then Jasper turned to Bonnie.

'If they give this dance, are you going?'

'Of course. How else will I find out anything from Kerby?'

Jasper went back in the store, and she turned to Matt, her smile fading into a frown. She apparently still didn't trust him, and he wanted her to feel differently.

But he was grim. 'You got a dozen masked killers riding around out there. And you got a bunch of outlaws in the saloon. Plus a sheriff what don't care about nothin' 'cept his pay. And a cattle company tryin' to take over the valley. But there ain't no proof against anybody. And foolin' around with dangerous men like Kerby ain't gonna help.'

'Don't tell me what to do.'

'You're bein' pigheaded.'

'Look, Matt . . .'

He turned to follow her gaze. A wagon was coming into town with Stoney, Red Oliver's cowhand, driving it. Worried, Matt walked up the street to meet it as it pulled to a halt in front of the barber's. Bonnie and Jasper followed, the dog trailing.

Chip, the other cowhand, was dead in the back of the wagon. Red lay there with blood on his shirt and neck, barely conscious.

'They got ambushed,' Stoney told them grimly. 'Red's still alive, but he's lost a lot of blood.'

'You get a look at 'em?'

'Nope. I was back at the ranch.'

Matt was furious. He helped lift the grumbling Red out of the wagon and carried him into the barber's, who took them to a back room. With tears in her eyes, Bonnie helped clear off a table, and Matt placed the wounded man on it.

Tuck began to cut away at Red's shirt. 'Looks bad,' he said.

'Just fix me up,' Red snorted.

Matt swallowed hard. He couldn't stand there any longer. Bonnie was helping Tuck, but Matt stormed out onto the boardwalk where Abnauther was talking to Stoney by the wagon.

'Judge,' Matt said, 'this has got to stop!'

'Well, in the old days, everyone headed for the settlement for safety,' Abnauther said. 'Maybe you could gather 'em all in.'

'And let their herds stray and ranches go?'

'So what do you suggest?'

'I don't know. But I figure I'm as good a target as any. So if I can't convince Mrs. McClain to stay in town, I'm going to ride back with her. Then I'm going to Red's to look for signs.'

'Monet and Kerby were in the saloon since early morning. Crutz, too.'

'Don't need to be in on the killin' to call the shots.'

'Well, good luck, Matt. I wish I could drum up a posse, but there just isn't one.'

The judge turned away, and Matt went back inside to check on Red, but the rancher was still unconscious. 'Will he make it?'

The barber shrugged. 'Maybe.'

Bonnie following, Matt stormed outside and found Stoney alone with the wagon, waiting to turn the body over to Tuck for burial.

'Stoney,' Matt said, 'why don't you go over to the McClain's with me, and then you can show me where it happened.'

'Okay. I'll tell the doc.'

Matt went down to the store with Bonnie trying to keep up with him, the dog trailing. Jasper had finished loading the wagon and was stunned when told about Red.

'You'd be better off stayin' in town,' Matt said to Bonnie.

'I don't think I have to worry.'

'You had to worry when they run you off the cliff. Just because Kerby Driscoll's fawnin' over you don't mean he won't do somethin' desperate if he's pushed.'

'I'm going to the ranch.'

'All right, but Stoney and I are going with you.'

'We don't need you,' she snapped.

'Yeah we do,' Jasper corrected.

Matt mounted his roan and followed

their wagon, the dog trotting alongside. Stoney left Red's wagon and team at the livery for Red and rode along in the bed of the McClain wagon. It was evening when they reached her place, and she insisted on serving them more elk steak. Jasper was talkative, but Single-Foot was silent. Stoney was bashful. Bonnie was still unfriendly with Matt.

The men were then crowded into the little bunkhouse. Blackie crawled onto Matt's bunk and crowded him against the wall. The dog put his head on Matt's arm, and he liked it right fine.

In the morning Matt and the other men went to Red's place. After Stoney showed them where it had happened, he was sent back to McClain's with Red's horses to keep an eye on Bonnie. The ambush had occurred in a stand of aspen near the ranch. There were no signs except spent rifle shells.

Single-Foot stayed on the ground, leading his horse and looking carefully at every overturned stone and every bent blade of grass. He finally pointed east toward the Target ranch.

'That way.'

The Apache stayed on foot for some time and then mounted, but the trail they were following into Target ran right into a thousand head of cattle and was lost. Try as he might, Single-Foot could not pick it up again, nor could Blackie sniff through the tracks. The Apache and Jasper went back to the McClain ranch, and Matt headed for town.

* * *

On the Target spread that night, Kerby was confronting his sister and father in the parlor.

'I thought you were givin' a dance for Matt,' Kerby said.

'But for that woman to come, it's unseemly,' Adriane said. 'She's only been widowed a short time.'

'But you count the men in this valley, there's maybe two hundred. You count the women, there's only twelve, includin' you.'

'If she's a lady,' Adriane said, 'she won't come.'

'Pa, talk to her. I'm crazy about Bonnie.'

His words hung in the air, and he paled. King Driscoll was glowering and staring into the fire. Adriane was uneasy, fidgeting with the lace on her dress.

'Well, look at it this way,' Kerby said. 'If I don't marry her, Matt Landry will.'

Adriane drew herself up. 'What are you saying?'

'Maybe he don't know it yet, but he's fallin' for her.'

Her face was hot and burning. 'He's in love with me.'

'You ain't givin' him what he wants.'

'And that is?'

'He's wearin' that badge like a halo.'

She sniffed. 'Of course, if that's what he really wants, he can have that silly old thing.'

Kerby snickered. 'Yeah, I can just see

you sittin' and waitin' for him months on end. You and a dozen kids.'

'Don't you talk to me that way. Father, stop him.'

'One way to get the McClain ranch is to marry it,' Kerby insisted. 'And I can be real charming on the dance floor. If anyone comes, that is.'

'Of course, they'll come,' Adriane said. 'All of them.'

'You want everyone to come?' King asked. 'Are you saying, you want the likes of Monet in this house?'

'Father, there are not that many people in this valley. They need to see the difference between us and them. Besides, Monet is educated and a gentleman, whether or not he wears that gun. And right now, I'm going up to make a list.'

She moved out of the parlor and up the stairs, while King looked up at Kerby. 'Sit down, son.'

Kerby made a face. 'What now, Pa?'

'We've moved twice, son. Once from Ohio, and before that, from Tennessee.

Now you're after another woman.'

'This is different. All I want is to marry her.'

King studied his son as worry lines creased his brow. His mouth was tight as he considered Kerby's smile.

'And that's all?'

Kerby nodded with insistence. 'That's all.'

'What about McClain's first wife?'

Kerby was nonchalant. 'I don't know nothin' about her.'

But King looked into the fire. He didn't believe his son.

7

Back in town Matt found Red sitting on a bench in front of the hotel, his right arm in a sling, bandages all over his head and chest. Matt dismounted and walked over to him, Blackie trailing.

'You're a sight,' Matt said.

'Well, they caught me when I wasn't lookin'.'

'Molly takin' care of you?'

'All the time, drat it.'

'I think I'd better have a look at the other ranches, see what's been goin' on out there.'

Red looked around. 'Where's Stoney?'

'At the McClain's.'

'Good. I'll ride out with you. I got to get away from that woman.'

And so it was that Red and Matt traveled the vast reaches of the valley. The other ranchers had not been touched, and there was no trouble. It was two weeks before they got back to the McClain's, and Bonnie was waiting in the doorway, a letter in hand, her face sober.

'An invitation,' she said. 'To your party.'

Matt took it, staring at the printed announcement. It was a dance in his honor. Although it didn't say it right out, he knew Adriane was going to announce their betrothal. He wasn't too happy about that.

Bonnie looked annoyed. 'It says the whole valley is invited.'

Red shook his head. 'That means Monet and his boys. I don't like it.'

After supper Matt walked in the cold night air while the other men bunked in the shack nearby. He paused at the corral where his roan was pacing. Blackie was at Matt's heels. He leaned on the fence and turned to look at the house, seeing Bonnie on the steps.

Now she was coming toward him in the moonlight, and he felt his chest tighten as she joined him. Refusing to look at him, she leaned on the fence.

'Why are you out here all alone, Matt?'

'I was just thinking.'

'About Adriane?'

'About the killings.'

'What have the Driscolls said about it?'

'They say they don't know anything.'

She frowned, tapping her fingers. 'Do you have family, Matt?'

'My brothers. And my folks are back in Kentucky and still raising horses. What about you?'

'My mother's a widow back in Missouri. She was a friend of Will's family. She's the one who wrote the letter that asked Will to marry me.'

'Why?'

'I just couldn't fall in love with anyone. She thought there was something wrong with me.'

'Was there?'

'No, I was searching for something. I thought I would find it out here.'

'But you never had a chance to find out.'

She pushed away from the fence. 'I'm not trained for this life, Matt. I grew up in a town where I never got my shoes muddy. I never had to walk in the rain without an umbrella. I learned to cook and sew, and I did learn to ride. But here I am in the wilderness, and I can't even fire a rifle.'

'Get Jasper to teach you. Soon.'

She turned, her eyes glistening in the moonlight as she gazed at him. 'I've been rude to you, Matt, but I can't help it. I had only known Will for a few hours, and then he was yanked out of my life in the most brutal way. I look at that badge, and I see Driscoll written all over it.'

'Well, you're wrong.'

'I hope so, Matt. Good-night.'

He swallowed. 'Good-night.'

She gazed at the silver gleaming on his vest and touched the star with her fingertip. The sensation bounced all the way to his boots.

She turned and headed back for the house while he gazed into the night, confused and uneasy.

In the morning Stoney and Red headed back to Red's place with their horses. Jasper and Single-Foot were in the corral as Matt saddled his roan. He looked up to see Bonnie on the porch. After he mounted, he rode over to her.

He leaned on the pommel. 'You got a party dress?'

'Just my wedding gown. I can make it over.'

'Save me a dance.'

She stared at him, her face sober and frozen.

As Matt rode away with his dog trailing Jasper came up onto the porch. 'Somethin' wrong?'

'Do you trust him, Jasper?'

'With my life.'

'He's the first man I ever — '

Her voice fell off, and she went back into the house.

* * *

A week later at Target, party plans were going strong. The grand hall in the back of the house was decorated, and Adriane was in her glory, ordering Lenny about.

In the parlor King and Kerby conferred.

'So Pollard's got the herd holding just south of Wrangler,' King said. 'That means tomorrow night, everyone in the valley will be here, and Crutz is on his way to tell Pollard to move in and take over McClain's and Oliver's place and burn everything down. With over five thousand head on their grass, there won't be anything they can do.'

'So they won't have anything to go back to. That means Bonnie's got to depend on me.'

* * *

The following evening, on the way to the party in the wagon with Jasper, Bonnie was worried. Dressed in her wedding gown, now trimmed in blue velvet, she felt out of place.

'I'm not sure I'll fit in,' she complained.

Jasper reached over and touched her hand. 'Don't you worry none, Mrs. McClain. They'll treat you right. I'll see to it. But you watch out for Kerby. I don't trust him. And I always wondered if he had somethin' to do with the first Mrs. McClain.'

She stared at him in the moonlight. 'What?'

'You ever learn how she died?'

'No.'

'She was found at the bottom of the canyon. Some man had put his hands on her, and then he had beaten her to death.'

Bonnie caught her breath, her hand to her face. 'You think it was Kerby?'

'All I know is, he was sure wantin' her. And now he wants you.'

'You're trying to frighten me.'

'I just want you to be careful.'

She shivered as the moon disappeared behind the clouds, and she drew her cape more closely about her. 'Now you do have me worried.'

'Nothin's going to happen at the dance. But since they're only puttin' up the women while the men sleep in the barn, the only men in the house will be the Driscolls and Matt Landry.'

'Matt's one of them now.'

'I ain't so sure.'

While the McClain wagon and all of the valley, except for Single-Foot who had stayed on the ranch with Blackie, headed for the Driscoll house, Matt was already there. And Adriane was having a fit.

She stood in the parlor with tears in her eyes.

'Matt, I can't believe you left your nice clothes in Cheyenne.'

'Couldn't bring all that on horseback.'

'But you should have told me. Now we've got to fit you in one of my father's suits. Lenny can only do so much in a few hours. Matt, how could you do this to me?'

'But you'll look pretty enough for both of us.'

She brightened a little. 'All right, Matt. I guess I just can't be angry with you. Now go on up to your room, and I'll send Lenny with some things to choose from.'

'Adriane, we have to talk.'

'What is it this time?'

He felt shivers run through him, and he turned to look down at the crackling fire in the stone hearth.

'I think we're making a mistake.'

'What?'

'We're rushing into this.'

'Matt, I know you've been different since you came here, but — '

He turned slowly. 'Don't announce anything to-night.'

She stared at him. 'Are you mad?'

'Just introduce me as a guest, that's all.'

His mouth was so dry it was painful, and he knew her rising anger was going to be directed at him in a split second. He felt sweat all over him.

Just then, King Driscoll walked in and paused.

'What is it, Adriane?'

'This, this man! He doesn't want to announce our betrothal.'

King seemed amused. 'Cold feet, Landry?'

'I just think if it's a mistake, we ought to figure that out before we say anything.'

'He's right, Adriane.'

'You're embarrassing me again, Matt Landry.'

'No, he's not, honey. Listen, back in Cheyenne, you were in a social whirl. Matt's just a little confused out here where it's all different. And if it's a mistake, you'll want to know it before anyone else.'

'How can you take his side, Father?'

'I don't want an announcement followed by a retraction. Do you, honey?'

'No, of course not.'

'Then let's take it a step at a time.'

She drew herself up. 'Very well, Matt.

But what my father says had better be the reason. If it has anything to do with Mrs. McClain, she's a dead woman.'

And Adriane turned, stalking out of the room.

Matt drew a deep breath and wiped his brow and face with his bandanna. 'Thanks, Mr. Driscoll.'

'I didn't do it for you. I'm not sure of you, Matt, and I don't want my daughter hurt.'

Matt nodded, hat in hand, and he headed for the stairs. He didn't want any mistakes either.

Up in his room he hooked his hat on the coatrack and felt strange relief, but he wasn't out of the woods yet.

When Lenny brought the clothing and laid everything out on the bed and chairs, he spoke just as she was to leave.

'Lenny, did you know there's a young cowhand over at the Oliver ranch?'

'So I've been told.'

'Aren't you interested?'

She put her nose in the air. 'Why should I be?'

'He'll be here tonight, you know.'

Lenny's eyes went wide. 'What?'

'Yes, he'll be one of the guests.'

'Oh, my.'

'And you have a smudge on your apron.'

She flushed. 'So I do. Thank you, Marshal.'

He grinned as she backed hurriedly out of the room.

But then Lenny made a mistake. She went to Adriane's room and spoke boldly of the cowhand Stoney. Adriane ignored her as she fussed with a gown.

'Miss Adriane, could I dance tonight?'

'Of course not.'

'But I'll serve and everything. I just want to dance with him.'

'You're a fool, Lenny. The answer is no.'

'But I — '

'Thirteen years, and you people haven't learned that nothing's changed.'

'All I want to do is dance.'

'What makes you think I'll even allow

this Stoney inside the house? He certainly has no social position.'

'Does Kid Monet?'

Adriane was angry. 'I don't want to hear another word. If you want to keep your job, go back to help Mr. Landry.'

Lenny stiffened, fire in her eyes. 'Yes, Ma'am.' And she backed out of the room to hide her fury.

8

As the guests began to arrive Matt was nervously being fitted in a suit a little small for him. Adriane was flushed with the color of her red silk gown and was being the perfect hostess. Two ranch hands were there with fiddles for the music.

Of the sixty odd riders of the Target Cattle Company, only a handful had been invited. But Monet and his men, along with Fowler and the sheriff, were there. The ranchers and merchants came in their Sunday best, all a little leery of the Driscolls but mostly there because of Matt Landry.

It was starting to rain, so Adriane frantically escorted the ladies inside, all twelve of them.

There was Molly, short and round, bubbling in a red gown, her eyes on Red while Abnauther watched her with adoring gaze. Two merchants in town had wives, and they both came. There were nine women from the surrounding ranches, some a little worn and weary, all married and some with small children they bedded down upstairs in the mansion.

The only single adult women were Molly and Adriane and Lenny, and Bonnie McClain.

When Adriane saw Bonnie for the first time, her fury rose, for she had never expected anyone so beautiful. She smiled over gritted teeth with her face burning and welcomed Bonnie, but she turned to glare up the steps, waiting for Matt to show his face.

Kerby rushed to take Bonnie's hand, and she was cordial to him, wanting to learn all she could this night.

Stoney looked bored at the entrance, but he finally came inside. He helped himself to some punch and turned to look straight at the pretty young Lenny as she put napkins next to him. His knees turned to water.

'So you're Lenny,' he said.
'And you're Stoney.'
'I don't like it in here.'
'Neither do I.'
'It's gonna rain, but there's a veranda out there, and we could dance.'
She tried to be aloof. 'Why should we?'
'Because I'm beautiful.'
Lenny laughed. 'All right, but later. I don't want to lose my job. Miss Driscoll's a dreadful woman, and they don't pay me much, but I'm not going hungry for anybody.'
As Lenny swept away with a smile Matt was coming down the stairs gingerly. He saw Adriane maneuvering the last of the guests into the grand hall, and he followed.
She turned and took his hand. 'Matt, you look just fine.'
He was surprised at her sudden sweetness. 'It's a tight fit.'
'You look wonderful. I'm very proud of you.'
Now she took his arm and marched

him into the crowd, silently proclaiming he belonged to her. It was then that Matt saw Bonnie. How gorgeous she looked. But she was on Kerby's arm.

The two fiddlers began with a waltz.

'You and I first, Matt,' she said.

'But we ain't announcin' anything.'

'You're the guest of honor. Come along.'

Matt was embarrassed, but he let Adriane drag him into the center of the dance floor. He took her in his arms, and they began to sway to the music. He had learned to dance well, and her smile said she was proud of him. He was feeling right guilty about trying to break off with her.

Then the others joined in, Kerby dragging Bonnie onto the floor and into his embrace. It wasn't long before Monet cut in, and then Fowler. Bonnie was nice to them all, hoping to learn something.

But King was looking at his fine gold watch. Any minute now, the new herd would be heading past Wrangler enroute to take over the McClain and Oliver spreads. Buildings would burn tonight. But he worried about the rain and went out into his office to peer out the window.

Kerby joined him there. 'Did you see her, Pa? Have you ever seen anyone so beautiful? Her hair is like yellow gold. I've got to marry her.'

'And if she says no?'

'She'll say yes.'

King was uneasy. 'Well, you have a lot to offer.'

'You think the cattle are moving on her place right now?'

'Yes.'

'Then she won't have anything left. She'll have to come to me.'

'Or Landry?'

'He don't have a chance with her. It's me, Pa. Me, she wants. I saw the way she looks at me. That smile. She don't smile at anyone else that way.'

Inside, Matt was dancing with one of the ranchers' wives, while Adriane swayed with a merchant. It was a slow dance, and Matt had a chance to look for Bonnie. She was dancing with Monet, who was holding her close.

'Mrs. McClain,' Monet said softly, 'you remind me of all the finer things I left behind in New York.'

Out on the side veranda Lenny and Stoney were dancing and laughing while Adriane looked around frantically for her. Then they rested against the railing and gazed into the soft dark rain.

'Where'd you come from?' Stoney asked.

'New Orleans. Miss Driscoll wanted someone who could speak French so she could practice. But I'm saving my money so I can get out of this house.'

'You've been to school?'

She nodded. 'Have you?'

He frowned, hands clasped together. 'No. I worked all my life down on a ranch in Texas. Came up here with a herd. Got a job with Red Oliver. But I want my own place. And Red allowed as how he would help me.'

Lenny moved a little closer. 'I'll teach

you your letters, if you like.'

'I like.'

Rain was falling gently around the mansion. The horses and teams had been put in the barn. Hours passed.

Inside, Matt finished a dance with Adriane, just as he saw Bonnie pull away from Kerby again. He came over to her with a lump in his throat.

'Mrs. McClain, may I have the next dance?'

'It's spoken for,' Kerby snapped.

'Now, Kerby,' she said. 'I must be gracious to the guest of honor.'

Matt took her hand. It felt small and soft in his. He led her into the crowd of dancers and paused in front of her, gazing at the look of her. Others were dancing around them, but he just stood there.

'What is it, Matt?'

He swallowed hard, but the lump stayed in his throat. He took her right hand in his left, and she slid her left hand to his big shoulder. He began the waltz with practiced grace, but it had never seemed so fine.

'You're staring at me,' she whispered, annoyed.

'My, you're beautiful.'

Color rushed into her cheeks and she looked away.

He bent closer. 'But I guess everyone's telling you that.'

'I don't believe them.'

'But you have to believe me. I'm the law.'

She looked up, surprised, and her smile spread on her pretty lips. Then she looked away again as she spoke.

'When are they going to make the announcement?'

'They're not.'

'What do you mean?'

'We're puttin' it off for a while.'

Again she looked up at him, then stared as they danced, their gaze locked together. It was as if they were suddenly all alone with the music. Matt could hear his own heart pounding in his ears. His mouth was dry, his body damp under the tight suit, and his legs were becoming wobbly.

Monet was abruptly at his shoulder, trying to cut in, but Matt would have none of it. 'You had your turn, Monet.'

'And you're no gentleman,' Monet remarked.

Matt was grim as he spun her away from him.

'What is it, Matt?'

'Monet and Crutz claimed they was accidentally shot in the saloon. The same night your wagon went off the cliff. And Monet speaks French.'

She drew a deep breath. 'You mean they killed my husband?'

'I don't believe the story about horseplay in the saloon.'

The music stopped, and Matt stood with her in his embrace, holding her at arm's length and savoring how delicious she looked. Another song began, more slowly. Abruptly, Kerby cut in, dragging her away with him.

Matt staggered off by himself, and Adriane caught his arm. 'Matt, darling, you must come and try some of these tidbits I had Lenny prepare. You'll think you're in Cheyenne, I promise.'

Matt had no appetite. The more he saw Bonnie with Monet, Fowler, and Kerby, the more agitated he became. He tried to concentrate on Adriane. He spent time watching Molly flirt with Red and Abnauther, but his gaze always returned to Bonnie.

The exhausting evening ended around three in the morning. The women retired to their rooms. The men, except for Matt and the Driscolls, were out at the barn.

In his second-floor room, Matt couldn't sleep and paced often. He listened to the heavy rain and watched the lightning dancing along the horizon. On the trail he would be thinking of stampede. On his own ranch he would be worried about the cattle bunching up under trees where they could be a target for lightning.

But here and now he was only thinking of the trap he had made for himself with Adriane.

At first light he dressed and went out on the veranda to watch the rain and listen to the distant thunder. He could see the barn where the men were huddled in their bedding. He walked around to the front, liking the sound of the rain on the roof, the way it fell in sheets from the edge.

And then he saw him — Single-Foot, trotting toward the ranch house, his horse trailing at the end of his reins. The Apache had worn out his mount and was finishing the way on foot.

Something was wrong.

Matt went back inside and found his leather coat, then went back to the veranda and down the back stairs, holding his hat down in the wind.

Reaching the Apache and pausing in the rain, he had a feeling of dread just from Single-Foot's burning gaze.

'What is it? What's happened?'

'Cattle. Target cattle. Took over McClain's. And Oliver's. New herd. Twenty new men.'

Matt bit his lip. 'So it starts.'

Single-Foot nodded and looked toward the house.

'You saw the men close up?' Matt asked.

Again, the Apache nodded. 'I saw faces. Try to burn bunkhouse.'

'Where were you?'

'Up in tree. White men never look up.'

'So you heard 'em comin'.'

'Dog told me.'

Matt stiffened. 'Where is Blackie?'

'Don't know.'

Matt felt an ache in his chest. His dog was missing, overrun by a herd of cattle. That didn't set right. He swallowed hard, then spoke grimly.

'Well, if they burned a single board of the bunkhouse, that's arson. That's somethin' to arrest 'em for. Will you testify?'

'I speak. Who will listen?'

'You got a point, but we have to start somewhere. Was there any particular man in charge?'

'Big man. Big nose.'

‘All right. Let’s go get ’im. By the time the others are on their way home, he’ll be in jail.’

‘What’s going on?’

Matt turned to see Stoney approaching in a heavy coat, and he told him what had happened. ‘Get Red and Jasper, but don’t wake anyone else. And be careful. Start saddling up. Get your slickers and one for me. I’ll slip a note under Bonnie’s door to go to town and not the ranch.’

Hours later Matt and his friends were riding through the hills where cattle huddled under trees for what they wrongly believed was protection from the pouring rain and darting electricity. Bending to the wind the riders held their hat brims down. Slickers loud with rain, leather creaking as wet horses picked their way in the mud, the riders continued northwest toward Red’s place.

At midday they rested in the protection of rocks, their horses weary from the slipping and sliding in the mud. Rain continued heavy and hard, cold as ice with tearing winds. Lightning danced on the horizon. The sky was black, and they ached from the cold.

Suddenly, hail began to fall in chunks, and the men crowded back against the boulders.

'Blast,' Jasper muttered. 'My old bones can't take much more of this.'

'This hail ain't anything like they got up in Montana,' Red told them. 'Sometimes it gets big as your fist up there. Why, I was movin' cattle up there one day when the hail knocked em' right down to their bellies. Weren't no way we could get 'em up on their feet again. So we had to roll 'em the rest of the way.'

Matt grinned momentarily, but he sobered again.

They shivered and huddled with their horses while they rested, and then they moved on as the punishing hail turned back to rain. By late evening they were at Oliver's.

Cattle were everywhere in the pouring rain, some crowding around the remains of the sheds and stable. Red was furious. He wasn't even sure what happened to his own herd. The horses were gone. The ranch house had been gutted by fire, and so had the sheds, but the rain had kept the roofs and walls in place. And in every direction, cattle, mostly steers.

'Thousands of 'em,' Jasper growled.

'And they ain't fat,' Stoney remarked. 'They been driven hard.'

There were no hands in sight. They continued through the hills and across the roaring creeks. They fought their way through the mud with only the crackling electricity in the sky as their light.

When they reached the McClain spread, it was long past the middle of the night, and they reined up in the trees. The corral fence had been battered down, and the outbuildings, including the shack that served as a bunkhouse, were gutted by fire. Cattle were everywhere, mostly huddled against sheds or under trees, with no easy way to sort out the McClain herd. The horses were gone from the corral. There was no sign of Blackie.

But on the knoll above the rushing water, the little house was still standing. Smoke curled out of the chimney and was beaten back by the rain. Horses were tethered behind the house. Lamplight glowed through the wooden panes.

Matt stared through the water dripping from his hat brim. He was glad the house was still there — glad for Bonnie's sake.

'We got a problem,' Jasper said, wiping his face. 'How we gonna get 'em out of there?'

9

'No one's ridin' herd or standin' guard,' Stoney said. 'They're too blamed arrogant. So they're all in there. How many you figure?'

'Twenty,' said Single-Foot.

They studied the situation. Rain was so heavy they could barely see the house at times. They dismounted from their weary mounts, pulling their Winchesters.

'First,' Matt said, 'let's get rid of their horses. They won't hear us in the rain. Most of 'em are probably asleep. Jasper, you and Red stay here and cover us. Me and Stoney and Single-Foot, we'll do the job.'

'Be careful,' Jasper said.

Leaving the horses with Jasper and Red, Matt moved down the slope from the trees, Single-Foot and Stoney spreading out. The rain was beating them like a hammer, and they had poor footing in the mud. Their slickers were heavy and clumsy, barely protecting their rifles.

At the foot of the knoll water was rushing through the high grass. Inside the cabin the men were comfortable and warm and snoring away. That irritated Matt plenty.

He shivered as he started up the knoll around the side of the house. When he reached the horses, he found no sign of anyone. They were still saddled, cinches loose, heads down, reins tethered to a long rope that was tied to stakes at either end. Matt was annoyed, but it was a good sign. Men who didn't take care of their horses were liable to be sloppy in other ways. Stoney moved among the mounts, talking quietly to them, calming them, stroking their necks.

Single-Foot kept watch while Matt and Stoney loosened each end of the tether and started walking with the rope stretched between them. They gently led the sleepy horses in a wide circle and back down the other side of the knoll, then up toward the trees where a lot of the cattle were huddled.

Here, they quietly freed the reins and draped them over the saddles. The wet and chilled horses were coming to life and starting to balk.

Matt took the rope and began swatting them on the rumps. They took off for the trees at a sudden gallop, falling into a trot as they bucked and headed into the herd. The rain and mud muffled their hoofbeats. Cattle scattered to make room for the horses, then collected again.

'Now what?' Stoney whispered.

'I don't know,' Matt mumbled as they crouched on the back of the knoll. 'We got to separate 'em somehow. We just want the one Single-Foot can identify.'

'So what's next?'

'We can smoke 'em out,' Matt suggested. 'They're bound to be asleep. By the looks of the smoke comin' out, they got a roarin' fire goin'.'

'They'll hear us on the roof,' Stoney said, warily.

'Go get the others. And bring a couple blankets. And some rope.'

Leaving their horses in the trees, Jasper and Red moved to join them, Jasper carrying the lariats. Red had the blankets, and since he was the lightest, he was considered for the job. But there was no matching an Apache for silence.

So it was Single-Foot who began the climb from their shoulders onto the board roof. The rain muffled any sound he made, but Matt suspected there was nothing to muffle. At length, the Apache was at the stone chimney, draping the blankets over the opening, slowly and carefully, then tying a rope around the blankets to keep the wind from blowing them away.

Once the blankets were in place, Single-Foot slid back down from the roof. The five men lay on the wet grass at various spots away from the front and only door, peering from under their hats as they waited.

Soon they heard coughing, then swearing. They heard the men scrambling around and trying to open windows without success. There was more swearing.

'Put out the blasted fire!' a man shouted.

But smoke was filling the cabin too fast, and suddenly, the front door swung open. A thin man in red underwear and boots began swearing and gasping. Smoke billowed out behind him.

'You fool!' another man shouted. 'You just flared it up again.'

Men started to come out now, most of them dressed and holding their slickers over their heads. All of them were cussing.

'Who was watchin' the blamed fire?' one growled.

'George was. Hey, George, get out here.'

A big man stumbled out, coughing and spitting and cussing. He had long skinny legs, scrawny arms, a shaggy beard, and was fully dressed, but unarmed. In the light from the smokey doorway he turned to snarl at the cabin, and they saw his big nose.

Single-Foot lifted a hand and signalled.

Matt counted. All twenty were outside.

One of the men turned to George. 'Blast you, Pollard, weren't you payin' attention? Look what you done.'

Matt swallowed. Pollard, Big-Nose George Pollard, the outlaw leader who had run the hideout in this valley before Driscoll and the others came. Monet and Crutz worked with him, and they all worked for Driscoll.

'Don't you be ridin' me,' Pollard snapped. 'I was asleep. And it wasn't my turn nohow.'

One of the cowhands laughed out loud. 'Hey, we finally got George to take a bath.'

The other men laughed, and one danced in the rain as the rest of the men came outside to join in the fun.

Matt sprang to his feet, and his companions followed suit, rifles aimed at the dancing, startled men. He shouted through the noisy rain.

'Hands up! U.S. Marshal!'

'What the?' George snapped, and he slapped at his side, but his gun belt wasn't there.

All twenty prisoners stood in the mud and beating rain, lowering their slickers and looking plenty foolish. Only two were armed, but they willingly dropped their gun belts.

'Now,' Matt shouted, 'back to back. Two at a time.'

Slickers falling to the mud, the Driscoll men had to stand while they were bound tightly to each other. They stood in furious silence.

Matt drew back, studying the situation. What the devil was he going to do with twenty prisoners? Locking them up wouldn't do much, not with Driscoll having sixty other hands spread somewhere between here and the Powder

River. Besides, some of these men looked like cowhands who were tripped into the job, some still in their teens. And the jail would never hold more than five.

No, he wanted Pollard. The others would be around if he needed them. He took a good look at some of their faces.

First light was hitting the hilltops now, and Matt made a decision. 'Get one of their horses for Pollard, Red. I figure the rest of these men can stay here and get loose on their own, sooner or later.'

'Sure could use some coffee,' Jasper muttered.

'All right, but make it fast.'

'And fresh horses,' Stoney added.

'And get a chunk of board from the bunkhouse,' Matt said. 'Any board that's burned through.'

So it was. A grim Big-Nose George Pollard was leading the way back to town on his own horse. His hands were tied behind his back under his slicker, and he was grumbling all the way.

In the cabin the nineteen men were frantically trying to free each other. The fire was out, and they were cold. The rain still pounded the roof. Wind rattled the shutters.

Jasper, Red, Stoney, and Single-Foot were all on fresh horses and leading their own mounts. It was a long way to town in this devil of a storm, but they were feeling pretty good about it. Except that Matt was worried about Blackie.

Keeping the prisoner was not going to be any easier than holding trial. The charges would be trespass as well as arson, the malicious burning of the dwelling place of another. And in this case, it was the shack that Single-Foot and Jasper had called home.

While Matt Landry and his friends were headed to town with their prisoners, many guests were facing a second morning at the Target mansion. The rain had forced them to stay. Brave ones had left, but Bonnie had stayed because Jasper was not there, and she thought he would return.

Food was being served at the mansion. Service was in the grand hall on long tables. Coffee was plentiful. Adriane was in her glory, calling all the shots and bossing Lenny, who cast shy glances around in her search for Stoney.

But Adriane couldn't understand where Matt had gone.

Bonnie, too, was curious because his note had only said to go to the hotel and wait. Wearing her riding clothes now, her yellow hair tied back, she looked around the crowded room. A child was crying. Everyone was talking at once, and outside, the rain was pouring down.

'Mrs. McClain,' Kerby said, taking her hand. 'Can I call you Bonnie? It'd be so much easier.'

'Have you seen Matt Landry?'

'No, I haven't. Not since yesterday.'

'Or Jasper or Red? Or Stoney?'

'No, why?'

'They also disappeared, but maybe they went riding.'

But Kerby wasn't so sure, and he headed over to Adriane and his father, who were by the coffee pots. He looked around carefully and spoke in a low voice.

'Pa, where's Landry?'

'Maybe he's sleeping,' King said.

Adriane shook her head. 'I had one of the men check. He's not there. He didn't sleep here last night. I have no idea where he went.'

'His friends are missing too,' Kerby said.

King frowned. 'Come on, Kerby.'

The two Driscolls went into the parlor, and King closed the door behind them. Kerby went to warm his hands at the fireplace, and he danced a little bit, kicking up his heels and then smoothing his hair.

'It sure was a great dance, huh, Pa? Did you see me with Bonnie? What did you think, Pa?'

King drew a deep breath. 'Kerby, aren't you a little concerned that Landry and some of those men have been gone since yesterday?'

'Well, sure. I thought you'd want to know, didn't I?'

'And where do you suppose they are?'

'It don't matter, Pa. It was too late for them to do anything about Pollard. It's a whole day's ride to the McClain's. Did you see me waltz, huh, Pa?'

King put his hand on the mantel. 'Kerby, I've got a definite opinion on Landry. He's no fool. He went somewhere to do something.'

'But how would he even know? Everyone was here.'

'Except that dirty Apache.'

'You think he come and told 'im? But there wasn't time. Besides, Pollard was bound to have killed that old Indian. Anyhow, what's three or four fellas going to do against Big-Nose George and his men? There's twenty of 'em. You didn't worry yesterday, Pa. Why now?'

'Because they didn't come back, that's why.'

'Maybe they didn't come back, 'cause they're dead.'

'Listen to me, Kerby. If Landry isn't dead by now, we're going to have to take care of it. I see nothing but trouble from him. Monet claims to be fastest gun in the territory. A fair fight might be the way to go.'

'What about Adriane?'

'I'll send her back to Cheyenne. She'll find someone else within a week.'

'It's raining like a waterfall out there. Nothin' they can do right now. So let's go eat, Pa.'

Beyond the next door Lenny paused with silver trays in her hands. She had heard every word. She silently moved on to another room, then worked her way back to the crowd where she cornered Bonnie on the pretense of helping her pour the coffee from a near empty pot to another.

Bonnie listened to the young woman's whispers.

'All right, Lenny. Thanks.'

But later that morning as some of the

braver settlers headed for home in the driving rain, Bonnie had to allow Driscoll's men to hitch up her team. And she had no idea how to handle the horses.

Standing in the doorway under the roof's protection, she was angry with herself for not knowing how to do much of anything.

Kerby came to her elbow. 'What's wrong, Bonnie?'

'I wish I could do everything for myself.'

'Hitch a team? Hunt for your supper?'

She glanced at him. 'Is that so funny?'

He smiled, leaning closer. 'Maybe not. But a woman looks like you, she won't never have to hitch no team.'

'Well, I want to learn. I'll have Jasper teach me,' she said turning away. She did not want to look at the man who may have sent outlaws to her ranch and plotted the death of Matt Landry.

Molly volunteered to drive Bonnie to

town, and Bonnie spent a restless night in the hotel room in Wrangler. In the morning she looked out her window at sunlight dancing on water in the muddy street. The sky was clear, but it looked very cold.

She had breakfast, returned to her room, and waited. Surely Jasper or Single-Foot would let her know if there was trouble. They would come for her.

In the late afternoon she went to her window and saw riders coming up the street. They were still wearing slickers. In the lead were Red Oliver and Jasper, followed by a big prisoner with a big nose. Behind them came Matt Landry, rifle across his pommel. Bringing up the rear were Stoney and Single-Foot. All but the prisoner were leading horses. They all looked weary and tired.

Bonnie was so glad to see them, she pulled a heavy coat over her riding clothes and went hurriedly down to the street.

The men had reined up in front of the sheriff's office, and Abnauther came up the boardwalk from his office in a hurry. Other men were on the boardwalk now.

Bonnie lifted her skirt and crossed over the deep mud, nearly falling, and she caught up with Abnauther. They reached the men just as the sheriff came hurrying outside.

10

Jasper leaned on the pommel. 'Mrs. McClain, this here fellow and his men, they overrun your place with Target cattle. Burned everything but your house. Don't know where your cattle or horses are.'

Bonnie stood silent, staring at him in dismay.

The sheriff frowned. 'You got any proof?'

'I saw him,' Single-Foot said.

'But you're just an Injun.'

'He can testify,' Abnauther advised.

Stoney and Matt dismounted to get the prisoner off his horse. Red, Jasper, and Single-Foot left to care for the horses and to eat at the saloon. The sheriff was so nervous he could hardly speak.

'Wait,' Gordon said, working his mouth a moment.

'We got to use the jail,' Matt said.

'Well, why don't you take him down to Caspar?'

'We have a judge here.'

'Yeah, but — '

'You're afraid of Driscoll?'

Gordon swallowed. 'If you ain't, you oughta be. You go ahead and do what you gotta, but me, I'm quittin'! And I'm going fishing right about now.'

With that, the sheriff went back inside to grab some of his gear and all he could carry. When he came out, he was in a hurry, heading up the street to the livery.

'We'll have the trial tomorrow afternoon,' Abnauther said. 'Four o'clock. Over in the saloon. Only place big enough.'

'Where will you get a jury?' Bonnie asked.

Stoney frowned. 'Yeah, a jury. Most everyone around here either owes somethin' to Driscoll or they're scared of 'em.'

* * *

The big-nosed man scoffed and walked into the jail, Stoney pushing him along. Matt came to stand with Abnauther and Bonnie. She sure looked pretty in the sunlight.

'Who is that man?' she asked.

'Big-Nose George Pollard.'

The judge nodded. 'And the charge?'

'Arson. The shack Jasper and Single-Foot lived in was gutted by fire. Some of the walls were burned through. I brought the evidence. And we'll add trespass. They was camped inside the McClain house.'

'Well, I'm appointing you prosecutor, Matt.'

Matt glanced around to see the curious men who had gathered in the twilight. There were three women in this town, and he might just want them on the jury.

'Who's going to represent Pollard?' Matt asked.

'I will,' said a voice from the crowd.

They turned to see King Driscoll and his son pushing through the crowd. Monet and Fowler were standing some distance back.

'You know any law, King?' asked the judge.

'I'm his best bet, Judge.'

Matt objected. 'I may want to call this man as a witness.'

Abnauther folded his arms. 'Well, Tuck's a learned man. I'll talk to him and the prisoner. But listen here, Mr. Driscoll, it's my understanding your cattle have overrun the McClain ranch.'

'And the Oliver spread,' said Matt. 'Everything was gutted there as well, but there were no witnesses.'

'Now, do I have to issue an injunction or will you voluntarily remove those cattle?'

'Who's going to enforce it?' Kerby grunted.

'Never mind, son,' King responded. 'Don't you worry, Judge. I'll have the cattle moved. They must have stampeded in the storm. Maybe some lamps just got turned over and burned everything.'

'Get your men out of Mrs. McClain's cabin,' Matt said. 'And cut out the McClain and Oliver stock.'

Bonnie took Matt's arm. 'I have to talk with you.'

'Well, I'm mighty hungry. Come along.'

In the cafe, seated at a back table away from the noisy crowd of men talking busily about the arrest, Bonnie and Matt sipped their coffee as Stoney joined them. The three of them ordered steak and beans.

'The prisoner's locked up good,' Stoney said. 'And Red and Jasper are in there right now.'

Matt cut his meat. 'But there could be a problem tonight. King's not going to like having Pollard testify. On the other hand, it could be Pollard's expectin' some help if he's convicted.'

Bonnie could hold her story no longer.

'Matt,' she said in a whisper, 'Lenny

told me she overheard King and his son plotting to kill you.'

'I'm not surprised.'

'They'll use Monet. He's supposed to be a fast gun of some kind.'

Matt leaned back in his chair, savoring the looks of her, the flush of her cheeks, the worry in her eyes.

'Your ranch just got run over,' Matt said, 'and you're worried about me?'

Her cheeks reddened. 'I can't let anyone be shot.'

'Well, right now they got more to worry about than me.'

Stoney frowned. 'Well, ain't you gonna arrest King for conspiracy or something?'

'All we needs is an overt act,' Matt said.

'You think a jury in this town will convict ol' Pollard?'

'What do you know about the women around here? I think Molly would speak up loud and clear. What about the others?'

Stoney was thoughtful. 'The store-keeper's wife, she's a bit timid. And they need Driscoll's business. The other lady, she's in bad health. Lenny wants to keep her job, and I wouldn't wanna see you put her on the spot right now. Save her for that there conspiracy. You want women on the jury, you stick with Molly or some rancher's wife, if they'll come into town.'

'That's your job. You and Red spread the word about the trial tomorrow as fast as you can. Get Jasper to help you. We don't want to end up with Driscoll riders on the jury.'

'What about Single-Foot?'

'You keep him watching jail and don't let him out of your sight. Without him, all we got is trespass.'

After supper Stoney hurried away.

Bonnie was subdued, tears brimming. 'I never thought I'd have such good friends.'

'You're not falling apart on me, are you?'

She smiled and sniffed. 'I guess not.'

'You have a room here? Hang on to it. When word of this trial gets out, everyone in the valley's going to show up. They'll be coming to see what brand of justice we got, mine or Driscoll's.'

She leaned towards him, her soft fingers on his rough hand. 'You be careful, Matt Landry.'

He could feel her touch run all the way up his arm. The way her eyes shone like starlight, a man could hardly stand it. He swallowed hard and went back outside.

There was a full moon, and not much was going to happen without Matt and his deputies being aware of it. He could see Driscoll riders lounging all over town and counted at least twenty of them.

As he headed back to the jail he looked down at the badge on his vest. It had not parted him from Adriane, nor had his decision to give up politics, and yet their planned wedding was a mistake that had to be corrected. Maybe the trial would make the difference. The thought of the trial made him nervous.

* * *

The Driscolls had rooms at the hotel, father and son lounging in their room.

'This sure is a sorry fix,' Kerby said, stretched out on his half of the creaky, iron-framed bed. 'Maybe we ought to try to get Pollard out tonight, huh, Pa?'

'You ever show your hole card before you have to? Pollard may get off. Now, did you talk to him?'

'Yeah, but it wasn't easy with Red and Jasper in there, so I had to whisper. I told him if he don't get off, we'll get him out tomorrow night, one way or another. But Sheriff Gordon, he took off like a scared rabbit.'

'He didn't do anything. He was useless,' King said.

'Anyhow, Pollard's not going to get us in trouble. He won't say anything about you and me. As far as he's concerned, there was a stampede.'

'And what about the jury?'

Kerby smiled. 'I got the boys circulatin'. Folks have the word by now that it won't be healthy to convict Pollard. Plus, by tomorrow afternoon we'll have about forty men stationed around town.'

'That'll worry the jury all right.'

'That jail's got plank walls nearly six inches thick. And a solid roof. The only real windows are up front. What if we can't get 'im out?'

King shrugged. 'Arson's not a hanging offense. And it's a long way to the prison at Laramie. A lot can happen on the way. But to answer your question, if Pollard can't be freed one way or the other, we'll kill him.'

'You forgot something else, Pa. There's only one witness. If we can pick that Indian off before the trial — '

'No, I don't want to take any chances until we know the outcome. Our backers don't want any trouble for the company. Besides, who's going to believe an Apache? Pollard's bound to get off.'

'And what about Matt Landry?'

'We'll deal with him later. But he's a dead man.'

* * *

Down the hall Bonnie lay on her bed in the darkness, staring at the moonlight coming through the window. She thought of the first time she had seen Matt Landry. From agony and horror, she had looked up at his strong features and grey-blue eyes. He had gathered her in his big arms like an angel.

Learning that Adriane Driscoll had Matt in her clutches had hurt her. But when she met Adriane, she became angry, for she could see the woman was a vixen.

* * *

Adriane, arriving for the trial, had the same feelings about Bonnie. As her buggy was driven down the muddy street she was pleased to see Driscoll riders all over in doorways and alleys.

The sun was shining, and inside the saloon men were lining up chairs facing the bar, where the judge would hold court on a stool behind it. Every chair was instantly filled by anxious spectators, and soon it was overflowing. The only empty chairs were those set aside for the jury.

At the jail Matt and Stoney were in charge with Single-Foot standing against a side wall, rifle in hand. Jasper and Red were across from the saloon up the street, keeping an eye out for trouble.

Matt had arranged to stock the jail with blankets, food and water, and the supplies were heaped on a table.

'You think they're going to try anything on the way?' Stoney asked.

'Not likely,' Matt said. 'But if he's convicted, we'll have plenty to worry about.'

'No jury's gonna get me,' Pollard said

loudly, his hands on the bars, trying to shake them. 'I ain't done nothin'.'

'Well, seems to me,' Matt said, 'that you was sitting in Mrs. McClain's house, and that's trespass. And if you got your hands on anything I find out about, it's burglary.'

'I never touched nothin'. And there ain't nobody out here complains if a fella takes shelter from a storm.'

'But you also burned Jasper's bunk-house.'

'Well, I'm gonna say we come on the main house for shelter, and that's it.'

'Single-Foot has another story.'

'They won't believe no dirty Injun.'

Single-Foot straightened, his burning eyes sent such a message that Pollard backed away from the bars.

'Well,' Stoney said, 'it must be nearly four o'clock.'

Matt swallowed. He could feel the sweat trickling down his back. He walked to the door and pulled it open, then carefully peered outside.

The street was lined with Driscoll

men, all watching his every move. Any moment a rifle could bark, and Matt could be shot down. And so could his only witness.

He had to take them up the street past the barber's to the saloon. Maybe three hundred feet. But it looked like a mile. His mouth was dry, his face damp. He loosened his bandana and adjusted his holster.

Rifle in hand, he cleared his throat.

'All right. Let's move.'

11

The late afternoon sun was warm as Matt and Stoney brought the prisoner outside the jail. Single-Foot was on their heels, Winchester in hand. Piercing eyes were gazing around and behind them.

Up the street men parted slowly for the procession, and every one of the Driscoll hands was wearing iron.

Pollard, recognizing some of his companions across the street, grinned and shouted. 'Hey, boys, look at me now.'

One of the hands shouted. 'Hey, George. That'll teach you to watch the fire, all right.'

'Shush up,' said Pollard.

Laughter echoed, and Pollard was enjoying the show, prancing between Matt and Stoney. Any moment, shots could ring out. Maybe they'd get

Pollard on purpose, or Single-Foot, or Matt and Stoney.

But the procession continued, and men kept making way for them. Soon they were at the railing in front of the saloon where there was standing room only. Spectators gave way, and Matt drew a deep breath, then shoved Pollard through the swinging doors.

Everyone seated in the room turned to watch. They all had heard of Pollard, and they were a little afraid. Molly and Bonnie had managed seats in the front row. Next to them were Kerby, Adriane, and King. Monet and his friends were standing at the far wall.

Matt's mouth and throat were burning dry. He kept marching the prisoner forward, then shoved him into a chair a few feet forward of the first row and some five feet from the bar. Tuck sat next to the prisoner, while Matt and Stoney sat off to the side in two other seats. Single-Foot made room for himself to stand at the wall near Monet, who backed away with a snicker. Red and Jasper took up positions near the door.

Tuck was busy reading a book the judge had given him, and the murmuring crowd's excitement was obvious. It was the first real trial in Wrangler.

The judge came out of the back room and perched on the stool behind the bar. With a wooden gavel, he pounded for silence.

'Now then, this court is in session. And I will not stand for any interference.'

To Molly's surprise, she was the only woman chosen and cleared to sit among the ranchers and merchants on the jury. No Driscoll men were picked.

'Your Honor,' a man in the back complained. 'I seen this here thing down in Laramie, and the women had to cover their faces.'

'You're out of order, sir. And there will be no veils to cover that lovely smile.'

Molly beamed with surprise, and she fussed with her red hair, while the other men on the jury just shook their heads.

'Now, Mr. Prosecutor, bring the prisoner to the bar and state your charges.'

'Arson and trespass, Your Honor.'

Pollard pleaded not guilty.

After Matt had called Single-Foot and other witnesses and put on his case, burned board and all, it was Tuck's turn. He stood up. 'Your Honor, Mr. Pollard don't have to say nothin', and so we rest our case.'

But Pollard jumped to his feet. 'You ain't shuttin' me up after what they said. I got plenty to say.'

On the stand Big-Nose told much the same story as other hands about the storm stampeding the cattle, but now Matt could cross-examine.

'Mr. Pollard, who hired you to bring the cattle up from Texas?'

'Why, Mr. Driscoll. He runs Target. You know that.'

'And when you reached the valley and camped south of town, did you talk to Mr. Driscoll?'

'Heck no! Just that there fella there, Sid Crutz. He come over to tell us what to do.'

All eyes turned on Crutz, who was against the side wall, stroking his small black beard, his eyes gleaming.

'And he works for Mr. Driscoll?'

'Well, sure, you know that.'

'Just answer the question,' the judge said.

'And what did Mr. Crutz tell you?'

'Well, he told us where to take the cattle.'

'And where was that?'

Pollard frowned. 'You know where. You tryin' to trick me?'

There was laughter, and the judge pounded his gavel. Matt paced slowly back and forth, his hand on his chin.

'Your camp was south of town when the storm hit. It seems a good trail boss would have kept 'em bunched up. Why did you move 'em when there was lightning all around?'

'They got away from us.'

'A stampede would have taken the

cattle right through main street. No, Mr. Pollard. Your trail circled the town in the rain. The cattle knocked down plenty of grass and brush on their way and muddied the ground. All the signs are there.'

'Well, uh — '

'I don't understand, Mr. Pollard. If you can be so easily confused, how did you ever head up a gang of outlaws?'

'Cause I'm plenty smart.'

There was more laughter, and the judge pounded his gavel. Matt continued to work on Pollard, but the man had been rehearsed and would not change his story.

'All right, Mr. Pollard. So you're a leader of men are you? What about your trail hands? They follow orders?'

'Yeah, I'm the boss all right. My men always do what I tell 'em.'

'And you told 'em to burn the buildings on the Oliver ranch and McClain's?'

'Who, me? No such thing.'

'But you saw the fires inside the buildings?'

'Didn't see nothin'.'

'Your men don't follow orders very well, do they? Instead of burning the buildings down, they just got the insides.'

'Weren't their fault. It was rainin' — '

'You made sure you didn't burn the McClain house so you could get out of the rain, isn't that right?'

'I told you, I was smart.'

'Isn't it true you couldn't find your way up a creek? And you didn't even know you were at Oliver's that night?'

'I knowed where I was all the time. I built that there place before Oliver even — ' Pollard's voice dropped off, and he glared at Matt.

'Right now, you're only accused of arson and trespass. But just maybe you'll find yourself up for a charge of murder.'

'Murder? What for?'

'Some of your men may have

murdered Will McClain and two ranch hands.'

'I don't know nothin' about that.'

'But if you were their leader, they wouldn't have done anything without your say so, and if they committed the murders, then you're just as guilty.'

'Hey, they got paid for it. Not me. I didn't tell 'em to do no such thing. They didn't ask me nothin'.'

'So who paid them?'

Pollard stared at Matt. His mouth was wide open as his eyes went round. Then his eyes narrowed, and his lips curved downward at the corners. 'I didn't mean that. I don't know nothin'.'

'When your men draw their pay, who pays them?'

'Well, King Driscoll, sure. He's the Target Cattle Company. You know that.'

Matt could get nothing more from him, and at length, the trial was finally concluded. King was squirming but managed a satisfied smile.

But before the jury was given the case, Tuck stood up, book in hand.

'Your Honor, sir, it don't seem like this here defendant has got that there competent counsel. And maybe this here ain't no fair trail.'

'Your objection is noted.'

Then the judge gave the jury instructions on arson and trespass, and they went into the back room while the judge kept order.

Within minutes they were back, and the foreman, a rancher, stood up to announce: 'On both charges, Your Honor, guilty.'

There was an uproar, and King Driscoll's face was dark but set with a practiced smile. Kerby was angry but clutched his hands together. Pollard could hardly catch his breath.

Abnauther pounded his gavel. 'The prisoner will rise. Mr. Pollard, you have been found guilty by a jury of your peers.'

'My what?' roared the angry Pollard.

'Counsel, restrain your client. Now then, you are hereby sentenced to the federal prison at Laramie for ten years.

Now since that prison charges the territory a dollar a day, it's likely you will be transferred from there to Detroit for incarceration. Marshal, take charge of your prisoner. I will prevail on the army for an escort. Court is adjourned.'

Pollard was steaming, his face red with fury.

Matt and Stoney were sweating as they removed the prisoner and fought their way through the rising spectators. Red and Jasper met them at the door with rifles. Single-Foot followed, and they marched the prisoner outside into the darkness, moving down the street with Driscoll men ready to draw on them.

Dripping wet, Matt and his friends shoved the cussing Pollard along in the cool of night. As they neared the jail shots rang out. Red and Jasper, who were between Pollard and the riflemen, were hit bad. They fell wildly to the boardwalk.

Stoney grabbed the prisoner and shoved him inside the jail. Matt dropped to one knee, six-gun in hand, his eyes scanning the shadows and buildings on the other side of the street. The shots must have come from somewhere between the livery and the hotel, but the Driscoll men had spread out on the far side and were acting as if nothing had happened. Men came running down the boardwalk, Tuck among them.

Jasper was hit in the left side at the ribs and in the thigh and was bleeding profusely. Red had been hit in the left arm and had a bad crease on the side of his brow, leaving him dazed and unable to rise from the boardwalk.

Matt was burning with fury as he got to his feet.

Abnauther came to his side. 'See who it was?'

'No, you watch the prisoner. Stoney and me will have a look.'

The judge didn't hesitate and went inside. Stoney came out with a rifle in hand. Men carried Red and Jasper over to the barber's for treatment.

Matt and Single-Foot cut across the street warily, but they knew the men would be gone. They checked the alley and livery and found no one. Single-Foot pointed to signs that were lost back on the street where the crowd was still milling. They saw suspicious smiles on the faces of Target men.

King and Kerby Driscoll, Adriane between them, walked by as if nothing had happened. Matt was fuming. He stalked back to the jail, Single-Foot behind him.

'Find anything?' the judge asked, shotgun in hand.

'No, but I figure they was trying to hit Pollard.'

The prisoner gripped the bars, face reddening. 'Ain't true.'

The judge turned to him. 'Well, you let me know if you want to change your story. I would cut your sentence considerably for your cooperation. And I would give you immunity as to perjury.'

Pollard grunted. 'You're just trying to trick me.'

The judge went out into the darkness. Stoney put the bar across the door, and Single-Foot edged up to one of the narrow side windows.

Stoney peered out a front window. 'Red and Jasper are hit pretty bad. That leaves the three of us.'

'I don't feel too good about this,' Matt said.

'What about gettin' him to Laramie?' Stoney asked.

'If word gets to the fort, we'll be all right and just have to hold out a couple nights here, but there's no tellin' if a rider will ever get through.'

'You're all crazy,' Pollard said with a snarl. 'Driscoll will have me out of here afore morning.'

'Well now,' Stoney said. 'It seems to me, he don't care if you get out or if you're just dead. Either way, you can't do no talking.'

Pollard made a weird face and backed up to the wall, then sat on the cot and stared at the shuttered windows.

The street outside was bathed in moonlight. Lights gleamed in the windows of the hotel across the street. Driscoll men were still roaming about, and there were about forty of them.

Later that night Abnauther came with word that Red and Jasper were going to be lain up for a week or more but would live. 'I heard from the storekeeper that Driscoll's men came looking for dynamite, but there wasn't any. Just the same they took the only keg of black powder in town.'

'Black powder,' Matt echoed.

Stoney nodded grimly. 'Bombs.'

After the judge left, Stoney sat with his boots up on the table. Pollard was snoring on his bunk with an occasional whistle that was annoying.

Matt sat at his desk, savoring a cup of coffee.

'Matt, what are you gonna do when this is over?'

'Reckon I might hang onto this badge

until this county gets set up. What about you?'

'Well, I might get married. If'n I can get me a stake.'

'Think she'll have a no count like you?'

Stoney grinned and pushed his hat back. 'Yeah.'

They both laughed, then sobered. It was going to be a long night.

* * *

At the hotel lobby Bonnie McClain found herself alone with Adriane Driscoll. The cordial good manners from the party were forgotten as Adriane came over to her.

'Mrs. McClain, you realize my Matt is in trouble because of you.'

'Why do you say that?' Bonnie asked, chin up.

'Because your little place is so important to you, you just had to see that poor Mr. Pollard in jail. Now Matt could be killed because of it.'

'That's the problem with you Driscolls,' Bonnie said. 'All you think about is what you have and what you want. That's why my husband is dead.'

'Yes, he is dead, isn't he? So why are you after Matt?'

Bonnie paused, her hand on the back of a chair to steady herself as she gazed with increasing fury at this prim woman who was shaking a fan at her.

'Miss Driscoll, if you are so sure of him, why are you worried about me?'

'Because he has foolish ideas about giving up politics, and you're just the diversion that would interest him.'

'It would seem to me that Matt Landry has a mind of his own.'

'My dear Mrs. McClain. If you knew anything about men, you'd know they can be easily persuaded.'

'If that's so, why don't you get Matt out of there? Your father's men are going to kill him, and you know it. On the other hand, if you really have no control over him, he will stay in there and guard his prisoner. So let's see just how much he will do for you.'

'Are you daring me?'

Bonnie smiled dryly. 'Yes, I am.'

'Matt will do anything I say.'

'Then why are you worried about me?'

Adriane was getting frustrated. 'Mrs. McClain, I can see where you are sorely in need of an education. Once this is over, I will see to it that you are run out of the valley. You and your dirty Indian.'

'You're avoiding the issue. Will Matt come out of that jail just for you?'

'He certainly will.'

'Then if you love him, get him out of there.'

Bonnie turned on her heel and went up the stairs, leaving Adriane red faced and angry. Despite the argument, Adriane had allowed herself to be put on the spot. But Matt had come over two hundred miles to marry her. He would do anything she asked.

Two of her father's men made a chair with their hands to lift her across the muddy street. She then waved them out of earshot as she pounded on the door to the jail.

'Matt, it's Adriane.'

He moved outside, closing the door behind him. In the moonlight Adriane looked lovely, her shawl drawn about her. She caught his hand and pressed against him.

'Matt, I was very proud of you today.'

'You shouldn't be out here. It's dangerous.'

'Not for me, Matt. Now listen to me. You've proved you're a good trial lawyer. You're being wasted here. And if you stay in there a moment longer, you could be dead.'

'Do you know something I should know?'

'Pollard has friends, that's all.'

'Looks to me like the streets are full of Target men.'

'Matt, don't be difficult. You've done your job. Now, please, if you love me, you will take off that star and come with me now.'

'Adriane, I'm keeping the badge for good.'

She stared up at him. 'You can't be serious. You know how I feel about it.'

'I'm sorry.'

'I thought you loved me.'

'Like I told you at the dance, it was a mistake all along.'

'You can't mean that. You would own a big share of Target, Matt. And you'd have me. Any man would give his life for that. So I don't believe you.'

'It was a mistake, Adriane.'

'It's that Bonnie McClain, isn't it?'

'She has nothing to do with it. When we met in Cheyenne, I was ready to settle down, and you were so beautiful. My head was in a spin, I reckon. But when I saw you again, out here where I belong, it just wasn't right. And I finally realized it had been a mistake. But I didn't mean to hurt you, Adriane.'

'Hurt me?' she asked, incredulous and backing away. 'I could have any man I wanted, anywhere.'

'I reckon you could.'

'Now you listen to me, Matt. If you don't stop this foolishness and come with me now, it's all over.'

'I've been trying to tell you it already is.'

'So you're not coming with me.'

'No.'

'Good-bye, Matt. I won't even cry when they kill you.'

She gave him a fierce look, spun on her heel, and stalked into the street, two of Driscoll's men joining her and helping her back across to the hotel.

Matt, bathed in relief, looked around at the shadows in the moonlight. Clouds were covering parts of the sky. It was damp and cold. He could see men everywhere, watching his every move.

'You see them Target hands out there?' Stoney asked as Matt came back inside. 'They're armed to the teeth. And with black powder, they could blow us all to pieces.'

Pollard was shaking. 'What are you talkin' about? I work for Mr. Driscoll.

He won't do nothin' like that.'

Matt glared at him. 'Red and Jasper took lead that was meant for you. So you'd better settle down.'

Stoney checked his rifle. 'I oughta be out there.'

'No,' Matt said. 'I need you in here.'

'Not me,' Single-Foot said.

'You're probably the only one who could move around out there without being seen,' Matt agreed.

* * *

The Driscolls were pacing their room at the hotel with Adriane visiting and standing at the window.

'He's not coming,' she said angrily. 'It's all over between us.'

King paused. 'Well, he's a lawman, and they're all fools. But it's just as well. Matt Landry's not leaving that jail alive.'

She folded her arms tightly. 'What about me?'

'Cheyenne, honey, is a bustling city;

remember? You'd have it at your feet again, and men will be begging for your favors. Or have you forgotten how it was?'

'No, but it's Matt I wanted.'

'Look at it this way, honey. Pollard's bound to try to make a deal, and he knows too much. We could lose everything. We've got to either get him out or kill him, and Matt Landry's in the way. You want to give up all your finery while I'm locked in prison?'

It wasn't hard for King to convince her she'd rather have her luxury than Matt Landry.

As the night wore on, Matt and Stoney stayed in the jail while Single-Foot was prowling somewhere in the night.

About three in the morning, it was plenty cold. Matt was thirsty for coffee and started the fire again. The lamp was burning low and hung near the jail cell, keeping the glow on Pollard. Stoney was sitting with his feet on the table, dozing off and on, while Pollard paced.

'Listen here, Marshal, sooner or later, they're gonna come to get me out.'

'They don't want you, Pollard. They just want you dead. And it's a long way to Laramie. Lots of places for ambush.'

'You're lyin'.'

'If you want to appeal your case and get out of prison in a hurry, you'd be better off with the truth. I can take you to the judge right now, if you want. You can recant your testimony.'

'Listen,' Stoney whispered. 'I hear somethin'.'

12

There was a tapping on the jail door, and Single-Foot entered. They barred the door behind him. The Apache was grim.

'Man sent to fort. Horse came back.'

Matt shoved his hat back from his brow. 'So the army isn't coming.'

'I get 'em,' Single-Foot said.

'That means we got another night in this jail. But you be careful, Single-Foot.'

'White-eyes not scare me.'

Matt saw a bit of pleasure in Single-Foot's face, and he smiled. 'Let's go see the judge and get you a letter to carry. It'll be daylight soon.'

'Maybe they won't hit us tonight,' Stoney said. 'I mean, why should they be in a hurry? They know the army ain't comin'. They're just waitin' for us to head out on our own.'

Stoney was right. Single-Foot left town, and nothing happened. Daylight came with drizzling rain. Matt went out for a stroll, keeping his rifle ready and taking time for hot coffee in the hotel cafe with no sign of the Driscolls or Bonnie.

At noontime Matt returned to the jail, and before long Bonnie McClain appeared at the jailhouse door, a slicker over her riding clothes. Matt pulled her inside. She looked so pretty with wet glistening in her yellow hair, but he was worried about her.

'What are you doing here?'

'I wanted you to know what I heard.'

'From who?'

'Kerby Driscoll.'

'I told you to stay away from him.'

She smiled up at him, then looked at the glaring Pollard and the sleepy Stoney. 'Can we talk outside?'

'Ain't safe,' Matt said, leading her to the desk.

She sat in the wooden chair, and he sat on the edge of the desk, his elbow on his knee as he leaned down toward her. She sure was glorious to look at, and just being near her, he felt good inside.

'Kerby was bragging how you would never leave this jail alive.'

'Why did he tell you that?'

'I'm afraid I made him a little angry. He was getting too friendly, and I — ' She blushed. 'I mean, I told him if he didn't leave me alone, I'd tell you about it.'

'What else did he say?'

'Enough to mean everyone in here was going to die, including Pollard.'

'Hey, you're lyin',' Pollard shouted.

'You can't stay here, Bonnie.'

'I know, but I wanted to see if you were all right.'

She gazed up at him with mist in her eyes, and then he took her soft hand in his rough one. He pulled her to her feet. As he led her to the door, she glanced at the angry Pollard and the curious Stoney, who spoke abruptly.

'That Miss Adriane. She have Lenny with her?'

'No, I don't think so.'

At the door, as Matt removed the bar, Bonnie paused, her hand on his arm. He drew a deep breath and held it, staring at her golden hair and blue-green eyes. He wanted to kiss that turned-up nose.

'God protect you, Matt.'

And she turned in to his embrace, her hand sliding up to his neck and pulling his head down. Her soft lips caressed his, and he turned to jelly. As she drew back he tried to swallow and couldn't.

Pollard shouted. 'Now ain't that sweet?'

'I think it is,' Stoney snapped.

Matt reddened as Bonnie backed away from him.

When she was gone, Matt finally swallowed.

'I wanna talk to King Driscoll,' Pollard snarled.

'No one's coming in here,' Matt said.

Later that day the men built a fire long enough to cook, also feeding Pollard, who was still complaining. And that night they all stayed inside. It was so cold, they took a chance on letting the fire burn in the small stove.

Rain beat noisily on the roof. Peering out the windows with the lamp turned down, they saw men still watching the jail. It was around midnight when a rock slammed against the front door.

They turned out the lamps and peered outside, and there was Single-Foot's horse coming down the street, reins trailing. Matt felt a tightness in his middle as he barred the door again.

Stoney turned up the lamp. 'He didn't make it.'

'But if he did, he's on foot, and we're gonna be stuck in here a lot longer than we figured.'

'I don't like sittin' here and waitin'. Why don't we go out there and do somethin'?'

'There's more than forty of 'em,' Matt reminded him.

* * *

King Driscoll and his son were in the hotel lobby, standing alone near the window. King was wiping his brow, but he was smiling.

'Looks like they got that Apache,' Kerby said.

'I'll believe it when I see his body.'

'You ain't scared of an Indian, are you, Pa?'

'I heard plenty about them Apaches. An officer I knew told me they could outlast a horse on foot. Got big chests, like an elephant.'

'But this one's old.'

'I don't think they ever get old. Just meaner.'

'You're sweatin', Pa.'

'Never mind. Are the men set up?'

'Yeah, sure. They're making those bombs out of black powder. Got enough for three bottles. And they're usin' lamp wicks, but they're plenty scared of it blowin' up 'em when they light 'em up. You know, before they can do somethin' with 'em.'

'Well, they'd better follow orders. I don't want anyone pointing the finger at you or me. We got backers to answer to, and I'm not losing what we have because of any fool like Pollard. So he'd better be dead in a hurry. Him and Landry.'

'If it don't work, I got me a plan.'

King grunted. 'You?'

'Sure. I saw that Bonnie McClain over at the jail. Now ol' Matt's sweet on her. So I'll just grab her, and they'll have to trade.'

King grimaced. 'Sure, that's real smart. We'd both go to prison. Listen, son. We want to get rid of Pollard without any witnesses. That powder will blow open the jail, but the rest of the town will be too scared to come and look. So it can be over and done with in the middle of the night.'

Kerby merely smiled. The long night dragged on with the rain held to a drizzle.

Matt had his chair by the rifle slot that faced the street near the barbershop. With the lamp turned almost out, he could see men milling around on both sides of the street.

It was nearly three in the morning. With Stoney asleep, Matt struggled to keep his eyes open. He was thinking about Blackie and wished he was here. The dog had meant a lot to him, and he worried the herd had overrun Blackie, trampling him somewhere out there in the hills.

Suddenly, Matt stiffened as he peered out the opening. In front of the barbershop five men were moving toward the jail. The man in the lead was Crutz. He had a bottle with a wick dangling from it in his hand. Shielded by another man's hat, Crutz struck a long wooden match. It burst into flame, and he lit the wick.

The men were between the barbershop and the jail where the alley was some ten feet wide, and Crutz lifted the bottle as if to throw it.

Matt aimed his rifle and fired, hitting the bottle.

The explosion shattered the front of the barbershop and sent the five men reeling like rag dolls. It rattled the jail. The roar hung in the air for a long moment. Crutz and the others lay lifeless on the boardwalk and in the street. A light went on in the back of the barbershop as Tuck must have been awakened with a jolt.

'They ain't too bright,' Matt mumbled.

Stoney had jumped off his bunk and come to peer out the small opening at Matt's side.

'Hey!' the prisoner shouted. 'What was that?'

'They tried to blow up the jail,' Matt said.

Pollard was snickering in his cell. 'Your lives ain't worth a plug nickel.'

'Yours neither,' Stoney said.

'Well, it'll be daylight in an hour,' Matt said.

Stoney walked over to the cell, and

Pollard backed off.

'You're a dead man, Pollard. You just don't know it.'

'Quiet,' Matt said suddenly.

The men hushed, all eyes turned to the roof. They could hear boots up there, and the rattle of the tin chimney as the cap was being knocked off. Matt grabbed his rifle.

Matt had barely reached the door when he realized something was in the stove pipe, clattering down.

'Oh no,' Matt muttered. 'A bomb's coming down the pipe. Hit the floor!'

13

Matt dived behind the desk. Stoney fell to the floor and rolled over under the bunk against the far wall. Pollard, wild-eyed and frantic, curled up on his bunk with a whine.

The chimney rattled as something came bouncing down it, and then it split with a thunderous boom that shattered the room with black soot and devastation. The walls of the jail were pulled inward but didn't give. The wooden shutters came off one of the windows. The door rocked.

The stove lid flew up and clattered to the floor with the coffee pot. The floor rose up and fell. A chair was thrown against the cell. The ceiling had sagged and dropped but held, part of the chimney still dangling. Silence followed the deafening roar.

Matt had had some protection from

the desk, but he was shaking when he sat up. Stoney was crawling out from under the bunk, so rattled he was trembling all over.

Matt rescued a lamp and lit it, keeping the light low.

Pollard was sitting up on his bunk, pieces of the chair imbedded in his arm. 'Help me.'

Matt fought for control of his wavering body, and he went near the cell bars as Pollard came frantically over to him. 'Pull 'em out, Pollard.'

In agony, Pollard jerked the wood from his arm and was bleeding. 'You gotta help me.'

Matt kept his distance. 'Stand back, and we'll slide more water under the door. You can clean it up yourself.'

'I'll bleed to death.'

'Just press your fingers on it until it stops.'

Stoney came over with the water and delivered it under the cell door, then backed away. 'Now you see, Pollard? Driscoll figured he'd get you right along with us.'

Matt was grim, picking up the stove pipe and trying to piece it together. 'Well, there goes the coffee.'

Color drained from his face, Pollard sat down. 'Yeah, you're right. They want me dead. Well, I'll fix 'em, but I want a deal.'

'Come daylight, we'll get the judge,' Matt said. 'I think we can get you out in one year.'

'You got to do better than that,' Pollard insisted. 'I don't want to be in no jail with Driscoll or his men.'

'You got a point. I'll make sure you're in Detroit or somewhere else. I'll write it up. Can you sign your name?'

'Yeah, sure.'

Matt wrote it all down as Pollard talked.

'Crutz and Monet led the attack on the McClain wagon. They didn't know there was gonna be a woman on it, but they went ahead anyhow. And they had some of the boys kill Todd and Chip.'

'But you were on the trail for months.

How do you know this?' Matt questioned.

'Crutz was braggin' when he come to meet the herd.'

'Unfortunately, Crutz is dead. What about the homesteaders who were killed?'

Pollard shrugged. 'We was all in on it.'

'Who gave the orders?'

'It was always from Kerby.'

'What about King?'

'Well, he probably told Kerby what to do.'

'Kerby ever do any of the killing?'

'Nah, he was too busy having fun in town. Except that one time when he killed that woman.'

'What woman?'

'Mrs. McClain, the first one.'

'Who told you that?'

'I saw him do it. I mean I came along just as he was shovin' her off the canyon wall. Then he bragged about what he had done and how it wasn't the first time he'd showed a woman who was boss. From what he said, I figure he'd already killed a couple women afore he ever got out here. And he was right proud about it.'

Matt was grim as he wrote it all down. He allowed Pollard to read it and then sign it.

'Well,' Stoney said. 'We got one empty cell. What are you going to do, Matt?'

'Get the judge and get a warrant for Kerby Driscoll. Crutz is dead, and I don't reckon hearsay's enough to get Monet without a preliminary hearing. And there's only speculation on King.'

Stoney peered out the other small rifle slot into the moonlight toward the judge's office. 'Hey, Matt, there's your dog.'

Matt came to the opening and whistled. 'Blackie,' he called.

The dog was in the alley and looked at the jail, then wagged his tail and took off into the night. Matt was tickled that Blackie was alive. He went to the door and peered outside, but there was no sign of Blackie. Closing the door, he was worried.

'Somethin's up out there.'

A few minutes later Stoney peered out the rifle slot toward the barbershop. 'Hey, they're tryin' it again. They got another big bottle with a wick on it. This time, they're settin' it down to light it. Five of 'em, and not one of 'em's got the guts to strike a match. They don't know for sure why it blew up last time. Look at 'em, arguing.'

Matt turned out the lamp, came to his side and peered into the night, six-gun in hand. The five Driscoll men had their backs to the bottle as they argued over who was going to take a chance on lighting the wick.

Matt caught his breath. 'What the?'

He and Stoney stared as Blackie suddenly shot out of the alley. Before the Target men could turn around, the dog grabbed the bottle by the neck and spun, racing down the boardwalk toward the front of the jail. The startled men backed away and ran, fearing an explosion.

Abruptly, there was a scratching on the door.

Stoney caught his breath. 'Your dog's brought a bomb right to our doorstep.'

Matt hurried to open the door a crack, and the dog came trotting inside, carrying the bottle of black powder in his teeth.

'Blackie, put that down.'

The dog set the bottle in the middle of the floor, and Pollard jumped to his feet in dismay. 'Get that out of here. One spark, and we've had it.'

'Good thing you ain't got no smokes,' Stoney said.

Blackie's tail was wagging.

Matt knelt and scratched the dog behind the ear. 'By golly, you're alive.'

Blackie licked Matt's hand. Pollard was gripping the bars in fear as Stoney carefully picked up the bottle and set it in the far corner.

'Well, Blackie,' Matt said, amused. 'Seems like you stole this, all right. And you brought it as a peace offerin', eh?'

'What are you going to do with it?' Stoney asked, nervously.

'Sometime tonight, if it's dark enough, I'm gonna bury it right out there past the hitchin' rail. And if they rush the jail, one bullet oughta do it.'

'That stuff is mighty touchy.'

'Right now, it's about daylight. I'll go see the judge and get those warrants.'

Matt had to see the judge before something happened to the confession. He left Blackie at the jail and went next door to the judge's office where a lamp was burning. He knocked and was allowed inside.

'Heard two explosions over there,' the judge said.

'They tried to blast us out. Once from the outside. Then they dropped a bomb down the chimney. They come back with another bomb, but Blackie stole it right out from under 'em.'

'And you're walkin' around in broad daylight with no protection?'

Matt shrugged. 'Didn't want nothin' to happen to this confession.'

Abnauther read it carefully. 'All these charges, it almost sounds as if Pollard made them up. And yet somebody's guilty for sure. But this thing about Kerby and the first Mrs. McClain, that's pretty bad. You think you can arrest him with a town full of Target riders?'

'They won't do nothin' in the daylight with witnesses.'

The judge frowned. 'My rider didn't get through to the fort. They found him two miles out of town. And Single-Foot's horse came back. Red and Jasper are flat on their backs. You and Stoney are all alone, and you're stuck in there, Matt. Sooner or later they'll break down the jail.'

'If Single-Foot did get through, the army should be here today sometime.'

'And if they aren't, and you try to take any prisoner south on your own, they'll bushwhack you.'

'You're the one who got me into this.'

'Are you joshing me? You could

hardly wait to get your hands on that badge.'

Matt grinned. 'I reckon you're right.'

Matt stepped outside in the fresh morning air. The sky was clear, but the street was powerful muddy. It was cold and damp with no wind.

He paused to look up and down the street. Target men were lounging about, but none of them were making any moves.

Sweat was trickling down Matt's back. His stomach had rocks in it. Arresting Kerby was not going to be any picnic. He sure could use a shotgun, but the sheriff had taken the only one in the jail.

As he prepared to cross the street he moistened his lips, for his mouth and throat were so dry they hurt. Four Target men were on the hotel steps. One of them was Kid Monet, his face set with contempt as he rolled a cigarette. In his fancy vest he looked like a dandy, but his six-gun was resting in a cut-down holster. Now Monet was moving forward and into the street.

Matt, who was no gunfighter, grimaced and paused. He didn't want to die out here in the mud, and he knew Monet was supposed to be plenty fast.

'Marshal,' Monet shouted. 'You have my friend in jail.'

There was a sixty-foot stretch between them, and that was too far for accuracy, so Monet began to move toward Matt, his boots sucking mud. Matt stood on the boardwalk, his back to the judge's office.

Monet had the unmistaken air of a gunman on the prowl, his hands at his side, his movements calculated. He stopped some twenty feet away.

'I don't think you know how fast I am,' Monet said.

'You don't think at all. You're doin' King Driscoll's dirty work, and he's stayin' in the clear.'

'You won't talk your way out of this one, Marshal.'

'Pollard had plenty to say about you. When this is over, you're facing a preliminary hearing.'

'You got nothing, Marshal. You're bluffing.'

Matt glanced toward the hotel and saw faces in the upstairs windows. King was probably waiting for Matt to die. Matt was damp and chilled as he stood watching all around.

Monet was working his fingers. 'Marshal, I'll allow you to draw first.'

'I'm not fighting you, Monet.'

'You have no choice.'

'I'd rather see you hang.'

Monet sneered. 'You won't live long enough.'

'Just get out of my way.'

'We're going to toss a coin, Marshal. When it hits the dirt, you'd better draw.'

Monet signalled to one of the Target men in front of the hotel, and the thin, smiling man came forward, tossing a silver peso in his hand.

Monet sneered. 'My friend will toss a coin. When it hits the street, I will kill you.'

Matt swallowed hard. He couldn't turn away. The whole town was watching to see what he could do against a fast gun like Monet. Matt represented their only chance for law.

The silver coin spun high in the morning air, gleaming in the sunlight, twisting, then descending down toward the mud.

It landed with a splat.

Monet drew, but Matt's Colt leaped into his hand at the same time. Both men fired simultaneously. Monet's bullet singed Matt's left ear, and Matt's bullet slammed into Monet's chest, dead center.

Monet paused, six-gun in hand, trying to draw back the hammer with his thumb. He took a sliding step forward, black eyes wild and round, his mouth wide open.

Staring at Matt, he dropped to his knees.

Then he fell face down in the mud.

The thin man who had thrown the

coin hurried to kneel and turn him over, but Monet was dead. The man looked up at Matt's Colt and stood up, backing away with hands raised clear of his holster. He turned and hurried into the crowd.

'Matt,' the judge said from the doorway behind him. 'Are you all right?'

'Yeah.'

'I don't know how you did it, but you beat Monet.'

'I was lucky.'

'That wasn't luck. You got a natural speed.'

Matt didn't answer, his breath just now returning.

The judge looked around. 'They'll have to resort to ambush now.'

Matt looked around the street for more trouble. No one was moving, but everyone was watching. The Driscoll men were heavily armed and just waiting for word to fire.

Matt kept his Colt in his hand as he moved across the street toward the hotel. His stomach was churning, and he was sweating because he had just killed a man.

And because arresting Kerby would be even more dangerous.

14

Matt kept his Colt in his hand and went inside the small lobby of the hotel. There was no one in the cafe or lobby and no desk clerk. Coming down the stairs was King Driscoll, followed by Adriane, and they paused at the last step. Bonnie was at the top of the stairs in her riding clothes, and she stopped to watch.

Matt moved a few steps aside to have a wall at his back.

King appeared friendly. 'Heard they tried to blow up the jail, Marshal. Was anyone hurt?'

'No.'

Adriane forced a smile. 'Oh, Matt, I have to talk to you.'

He waved her back. 'Where's Kerby?'

King's face darkened. 'Why?'

'I have a warrant for his arrest.'

'On what charge?'

'He murdered the first Mrs. McClain.'

King went pale. 'That's a lie.'

'Pollard saw him do it.'

'He's lying to save his skin.'

Matt was grim. 'We'll let the jury decide that.'

'You'd never get a conviction.'

'Not here, maybe. But Laramie might be different.'

King's hands were shaking as he gripped them together. Adriane was frantic and took her father's arm.

'Matt,' she whispered. 'Don't do this.'

Her father drew a deep breath. 'Let me bring him down, Marshal. We'll talk to the judge.'

'Nobody's takin' me anywhere!'

The voice was cold and harsh and came from Kerby Driscoll at the top of the stairs. He had his six-gun in his right hand, and his left arm was around Bonnie's throat, choking her as she frantically clawed at his arm. He kept her in front of him.

Matt froze. 'Let her go.'

'You blast me, you'll get her,' Kerby said. 'Now stand aside. All of you. Me and the little lady are going for a ride.'

'You ain't goin' nowhere,' Matt said.

King pushed Adriane behind him as he turned. 'Kerby, put that gun down and let her go.'

'You made me run away from Ohio, and all the time, you know them women got what they deserved. And so did McClain's woman. Leadin' a man on for nothin'. Smilin' and teasin'.'

'Kerby, for my sake,' King gasped. 'Please — '

'No, Pa. You're always stoppin' me. Well, this time, I'm in charge. And I'm not running away no more.'

Bonnie was fighting to free herself, but she was too small in his strong grip. Every effort she made only cut off her wind, and she was gasping for air.

Bonnie tried kicking him with her boot, but he just lifted her off her feet, and she lost all her color. She was unconscious, and he relaxed his arm hold from her neck, letting her fall slightly. He then wrapped his left arm about her waist and held her in front of him.

Matt was hot with anger. He kept aiming at Kerby as the man came down the steps, dragging the motionless Bonnie with six-gun pointed to her temple.

Adriane gripped her father's arm. 'Kerby, stop this.'

'Let him go, honey,' King advised her.

'Yeah,' Kerby snarled. 'And you, Marshal, drop that Colt or I'll blow her head off.'

'No, you won't.'

Matt backed to the wall, six-gun leveled, but he didn't want to agitate the crazed Kerby.

Dragging Bonnie outside with his weapon still at her head, Kerby made faces at the men who turned to stare. He moved out onto the steps, then onto the boardwalk and into the street. The sun was bright, but the mud sucked at his boots as he continued his staggered path.

Bonnie, coming to life, found herself in the circle of his arm. She pretended to still be unconscious while held tight at his side, the barrel of his gun hard against her temple.

Matt was on the boardwalk, the Colt ice cold in his grip. He was in agony, not knowing just what to do next, so he just started walking toward Kerby, who came to a halt.

'Stay back, Marshal.'

Matt stopped some ten feet from them.

Suddenly, Bonnie reared up and clawed Kerby's face. He yelped, and she broke free, falling backwards into the mud and crawling frantically away.

As Kerby tried to chase her, Matt holstered his gun and flew across the space between them like a bullet. He crashed into Kerby who fired at him, the bullet burning Matt's left arm above the elbow.

But Matt was upon him, beating him down to the muddy ground. Kerby fought back, grabbing Matt around the neck and wounded arm. Kerby pounded his chest, and Matt slammed his big fist into Kerby's jaw.

They rolled in the mud, sliding around in their struggle to get a grip on each other. Matt rose up over him, then hit him on the jaw again. Kerby's six-gun was lost in the mud, and he roared like an animal as he slid out from under Matt. He got up on his knees and charged at the prone Matt, falling on him.

Again they rolled around, beating each other with their fists. Kerby kicked and clawed. They were both covered with mud, and each was slippery as the other tried to grab hold.

They rose to their feet, grappling wildly. Then Kerby lost his footing and fell backwards, landing on his rear.

Matt jumped forward and grabbed him, rolling him over and bringing his right arm behind his back with a crunch. Kerby yelled, but he was stopped cold.

'Hold it,' shouted Stoney from the doorway of the jail.

Matt dragged his prisoner to his feet and turned to see Blackie running out in the mud to his side.

Matt pushed the prisoner forward, and Stoney helped him shove Kerby into the other cell as Pollard backed as far away as he could. Kerby was so covered with mud, he was hardly recognizable. Matt was just as covered, but he could take a bath. His dog shook off its mud, all over Stoney, who swore.

'Get Kerby some water to clean up,' Matt said.

Moving back outside with Blackie trailing, Matt saw Bonnie sitting up in the mud. Beyond, King Driscoll held his daughter's hand on the hotel steps, and he was furious as he shouted at Matt.

'You can't hold my son. Not on the word of some outlaw who's trying to save his own skin.'

'Seems your son added a few words of his own.'

‘That’s not admissable.’

‘I’m afraid it is, bein’ spontaneous like it was.’

King looked devastated as Adriane hugged him.

Matt knelt at Bonnie’s side. She had mud on her face and clothes and even in her hair, but she smiled.

‘You look awful,’ Matt said.

‘So do you. Like greased pigs at the county fair.’

He grinned, taking her hand and pulling her to her feet. ‘I reckon we both need a bath and a change of clothes.’

She slid against him, and his arm went around her. But when she saw Adriane watching from the hotel steps she pulled away on her own, so he just held her hand.

Before they could reach the board-walk, Matt’s feet went out from under him, and he went over backwards. Bonnie tried to hold him and lost her footing, crashing down against his chest.

They collasped in the mud. Matt was disgusted, so he just lay there, soaking in it, while Bonnie sat up at his side. She was laughing at him, and he looked up at her. Even with her muddy face, she was beautiful.

He reached up to put his hand at her shoulder, and he pulled her down to him, forcing her face closer, muddied flaxen hair falling about her throat and cheeks. She looked delicious. His lips found hers but slid right off. They laughed together.

She drew back, and again he got to his feet. He took her hand and carefully pulled her up to his side. As his arm encircled her, he finally remembered the whole town was watching. His face reddened under the mud.

The Driscolls watched a long moment, then went back inside the hotel.

At the hotel entrance Matt paused, her hand in his.

'Will you be all right?'

'Yes, but, Matt, what are you going to

do? It's just you and Stoney in there. And they must have the town sealed off.'

'You just go upstairs and stay there.'

Bonnie nodded, squeezing his hand, and went inside, where she was instantly confronted by an angry Adriane.

'You stay away from my Matt.'

Bonnie's face darkened under the mud. 'I didn't kiss him. He kissed me.'

'Just remember what I said. He's mine.'

Bonnie turned and went up the stairs, and Adriane was smug, determined if she couldn't have Matt, neither could this useless woman.

Meanwhile, Matt headed for the jail to gather some clean clothes before going to Tuck's for a hot bath.

He entered through the barbershop through the gaping hole in front and went to the back rooms where he found a barely conscious Red and a heavily bandaged, immobile Jasper, both on beds against the walls.

Jasper was trying to talk. His words came with great difficulty. 'I'm right sorry, Matt.'

'Don't worry about it.'

'Tuck says you got Monet. And now you got Kerby in jail.'

'Stoney's in there with me. We'll be all right.'

But even as he had his bath and changed into clean clothes, Matt wasn't so sure. As he went back out into the sunlight he glanced down at the silver badge on his shirt, wondering if it was worth all of this. He knew it was.

Back at the jail Matt slumped in his chair at the desk. He was exhausted and weary, and as he checked his Colt he felt nausea from having killed a man.

Stoney was sitting with his boots on the table.

Pollard, keeping as far from the angry Kerby as he could, was gripping the cell bars. 'Marshal, you can't keep me in here with ol' Kerby.'

'Keep quiet,' Stoney said, 'or I'll gag you.'

Pollard glared at him and went back to his bunk, but Kerby sat looking at Pollard with contempt. 'When I get out of here, Pollard, I'll personally string you up.'

'Yeah, well, you're gonna hang, Kerby. I never did like you none. You're a dude, that's what you are. A nothing. And I saw you kill that first Mrs. McClain.'

'You're lyin'. And I can tell plenty about you.'

'You don't know nothin',' Pollard snapped. 'Besides, I made a deal, and it's too late for you.'

'Yeah, well, maybe the marshal would wanna hear about all them raids you made out of this valley afore we come along, and how we got you to bribe the sheriff, and how you were the ones doin' most of the killin'.'

'You gave the orders,' Pollard said.

Kerby hid his fear by sitting down with a mean look on his face, but he was plenty worried and sweating.

The smithy came and repaired the

stove pipe with new fittings so they could have hot food and coffee. Matt and Stoney took turns sleeping, for they knew there was a long night ahead. When Matt was lying down, Blackie came and crawled on the cot, settling down with his head on Matt's chest, his wet nose inches from Matt's chin.

'You're a thief,' Matt mumbled.

Blackie lapped Matt right across the mouth, and Matt grumbled and wiped his lips. 'Drat.'

That night they were on their guard. Matt had buried the black powder out front when the moon was covered by clouds, but he realized he'd have a hard time seeing it in the dark.

The prisoners were sleeping around midnight when Matt began to feel his skin crawl. Blackie was growling and hair was rising on the back of the dog's neck as Matt sat up, shoving Blackie aside.

Stoney sat up in his chair. 'Somethin's goin' on.'

They turned down the lamps, and

Matt peered out the front window into the moonlight. Men on horseback were gathering with a huge log dangling from ropes between two of their mounts. They lined up in front of the jail and were heavily armed. They were going to ram the door.

15

Matt pulled his six-gun. Maybe he couldn't see the bottle, but he knew where it was. He shoved the window shutter aside, and as the crowd of riders readied the charge, he saw a glint of moonlight on the neck of the bottle.

The front riders with the log between them spurred their horses to a lope, the other riders crowding behind. There had to be twenty of them.

Matt drew a deep breath and fired at the half-buried black powder, missing. He fired again and could barely see the bottle through the flying hoofs. He took another shot, missing again. But as the log struck the door with a loud crack Matt fired and hit the bottle.

The explosion lifted the animals and riders into the air and tossed them like kindling. The untended log slammed into the bottom of the door but didn't break it. The jailhouse shook, walls trembling, windows rattling.

Four horses were down, and many of the riders had been thrown. At least six looked dead or badly hurt, two of them crawling away. The others gathered their mounts and left the street.

'They'll get in here,' Kerby said loudly. 'One way or another, you're a dead man, Marshal.'

'You could be right,' Matt said. 'But come mornin', I'm takin' you and Pollard in irons to the fort.'

'You'll never make it,' Kerby said.

But Kerby fell silent, and Matt left the jail two hours before dawn. He went to Abnauther's office and pounded on the door. The judge came forward in his nightshirt as Matt made arrangements.

'Get me a wagon and two saddle horses before sunup.'

'This is crazy, Matt. But I'm going with you.'

As Matt left the office and looked up the street he saw three men on the roof of the jail in the moonlight. They had burning gunny sacks. Even with Kerby inside, they were trying to burn the roof. They were really desperate to get inside.

Matt drew his six-gun. 'Get down off there.'

The men rolled around and opened fire, and Matt fired back, then dived into the alley, flattening against the jail. Smoke was curling off the roof into the moonlight.

Matt looked down at his left arm and his thigh. Blood was spilling forth. He drew a deep breath as he listened to the scrambling on the roof. They were going off the back, and he slid along the wall, ignoring the shock of his wounds.

Then he jumped around the corner just as two of them hit the ground. 'Hands up.'

The men froze, slowly turning with hands still clutching their six-guns as they lifted their arms. Then one jumped aside and started firing. Matt fired back, hitting him dead center. The other man fired, and Matt shot him between the eyes.

He had hardly caught his breath when he heard something on the roof. He spun around, firing before the wounded man above could pull the trigger. The man lay half off the roof, arms dangling as his weapon fell to the ground.

Matt had two shots left, but he picked up the dead man's gun and shoved it in his belt. Leaning against the wall, he was beginning to feel the pain shooting through his left arm above the elbow and the outside of his left thigh.

Smoke was still curling from the roof. Matt believed the wood was too wet to burn and needed help. He knew Stoney was inside plenty worried, but the man had sense enough to stay there.

Matt moved into the alley between the jail and the barbershop. Instead of going to the broken front, he pounded on the side window. Tuck let him in and cleaned him up with bandages and a sling on his arm. He was glad to see that Red and Jasper were getting better even if they couldn't sit up.

Limping back to the jail, Matt was disgusted, but in daylight, he could see the sacks had burned to ashes without the roof catching fire. Before he could enter, he saw Bonnie waving to him from her hotel window. He waved back.

Inside the jail Matt sat at his desk and put his left boot on top of it. He was exhausted.

'Hah,' said Kerby. 'You ain't goin' nowhere.'

Stoney pulled up a chair by Matt. 'They won't give up. We got to do somethin', Matt, and you ain't in no condition to ride to the fort.'

'Wagon'll be here at sunup. We're goin'.'

And so it was that before sunlight hit the street, the dead horses and men were gone. The wagon was loaded for the two-day trip, Abnauther at the reins. Two saddle horses were tied behind.

The prisoners' arms and legs were shackled, and they were forced into the back of the wagon. Abnauther sat across from them, his fancy hunting shotgun aimed at their bellies. Matt climbed in with him, his pain shooting through him like hot fire. Blackie leaped in to lie beside him.

Stoney got on the wagon seat and took the reins, just as Molly came running up, eyes wide.

'Judge, what are you doing in there?'

'Goin' to the fort.'

'But you can't do that.'

Abnauther frowned. 'Why not?'

'Because — well, because you could get hurt.'

'You never worried about me before.'

'You never did this before.'

'You're busy with Red. Why bother with me?'

She looked frustrated, her round face flushed. 'I don't know. I don't never see you doing anything but look mean.'

Stoney headed the team down the street, then reined up.

Twenty riders were lined up side by side, six-guns drawn, blocking the street. In the center was King Driscoll, looking plenty mean in the early sunlight with a rifle aimed at them. Metal gleamed on the weapons. Every man looked ready to back up Driscoll.

And none of the town's citizens were interested in backing up the law. They were all hiding behind windows and doors. There was a heavy silence.

'Uh, oh,' Stoney said.

'You are not taking my son anywhere.'

Matt rose up as best he could, rifle ready.

'You men had better move, or you'll be under arrest for interferin' with a peace officer.'

Suddenly, Stoney grabbed the buggy whip and cracked it hard on the rumps of the team, and they broke into a lope, then a gallop as Stoney whipped them again, straight into the line of riders. Shots rang out, and Stoney was hit, but he kept going.

Matt and Abnauther were firing in all directions as the wagon raced down the street. Men fell from the saddle. King Driscoll rode right up to the side of the wagon and aimed at Matt's back, but Blackie barked.

Matt ducked and fired, hitting Driscoll square between the eyes. The rancher gasped, mouth open wide, then weaved in the saddle as his horse jumped aside. While Matt was distracted, another rider came up behind him. He was about to shoot him in the back when Blackie leaped from the wagon and landed on the man's pommel and forced his mount to rear.

As Blackie was thrown to the ground the man turned to fire again, and Matt shot him in the chest. The man spun his horse and fell from the saddle.

The other riders charged again, but Matt and Abnauther kept firing. As the wagon cleared the town the men had either been shot from the saddle or had discovered that the man who paid them was dead.

Blackie caught up and leaped into the wagon.

Stoney, bleeding from the shoulder, suddenly reined the team to a halt just south of town.

'Don't stop,' Matt said.

'Take a look,' Stoney countered.

Matt rose from the wagon as best he could, pulling himself up to the back of the wagon seat and resting on his right knee as he stared at the trail ahead.

Single-Foot was trotting toward them on foot.

Far behind was the shape of a cavalry troop, flag waving, some distance away. The Apache had out-lasted another horse, and now he was coming slowly to a halt in front of the wagon. He didn't seem out of breath, but his big chest was heaving slightly.

He gazed at Stoney with blood on his shoulder, Matt all bandaged, and Abnauther with blood on the side of his head. He looked past them at the carnage in the street.

'Single-Foot,' Stoney said. 'Am I glad to see you.'

'You make big mess.'

The Apache climbed up on the wagon to take the reins and turned the team around, heading back up the street, avoiding the bodies.

Molly ran toward the wagon, her face red, and walked along with it. 'Judge, you're hurt.'

Abnauther moaned a little more than necessary, and when the wagon pulled up by the jail, he let her help him down. She was bigger around but not as tall, and he leaned on her.

'Listen to me, woman. You've got to make up your mind. Is it me or Red?'

'Why, it's you, Judge.'

Matt and Stoney, with Single-Foot's help, moved the prisoners still shackled back into their cells.

Kerby was furious, having lost his father and his last hope of escape. But Pollard, no longer afraid of Driscoll, spoke up. 'I got plenty to tell you now, Marshal. Maybe enough to keep me out of jail.'

'You shut up,' Kerby snapped.

'Ain't afraid of you no more. Your

Pa's dead. And I ain't doin' no time if I can help it. I know all about how you was stealin' from your Pa. And them fellas what set up the cattle company ain't gonna be too happy about it.'

'Settle down,' Matt said. 'I'll let you talk to the judge as soon as he's fixed up.'

Leaving Single-Foot to watch the jail, Stoney and Matt went outside. Stoney, still bleeding, went up to the barber's. Matt stood on the boardwalk watching the army nearing town. His wounds hurt, and he was bone weary.

He paused to see Lenny coming into town on a sorrel. She was too late to see Stoney enter the barber's, so she kept riding toward Matt, her eyes wide as she surveyed the damage.

Across the street he saw Adriane and Bonnie on the steps of the hotel, but he waited for Lenny to ride up. He told her what had happened and that Stoney was at Tuck's getting patched up.

'I'll go see him,' she said, but she sat quiet in the saddle, staring across at the haughty Adriane. 'I guess I don't have a job.'

'Stoney figures you do.'

Lenny smiled. 'You think so? I'll go find out.'

She turned the horse back up the street, and Matt figured there sure enough was need for a preacher in Wrangler, but the judge would have to handle things.

He gazed at Adriane, the woman he had ridden two hundred miles to marry. And Bonnie, golden hair gleaming in the sunlight, blue-green eyes glistening as she looked from him to Adriane.

Matt limped across to pause on the boardwalk in front of them. Bonnie looked happy to see him, but Adriane's face was red hot, her voice caustic.

'You killed my father. I don't know why I ever wanted you, Matt Landry. But I can tell you this; I'll make sure you are never governor of this territory.'

Matt had to smile, for she had never accepted his disinterest in being governor. His amusement made Adriane so angry that she spun on her heel and went back inside. He had no evidence she had been part of the conspiracy to take over the valley, but he realized now she must have known what her father and brother were doing.

Bonnie, uncertain what was happening, came down the steps. 'I'm sorry, Matt. Maybe she'll change her mind.'

'We had already called it off.'

'You had?'

He nodded, and she was trying to frown, although a smile kept pulling at the corners of her lips. 'Why didn't you tell me?'

Matt was grinning as he pushed his hat back. 'I thought you'd figure it out when I kissed you in front of her and the whole town. Weren't you paying attention?'

She made a face, then smiled. 'I can see you need to learn some manners.'

'And you're going to teach me?'

'Yes, I am.'

'You can teach our kids when we're married. But you're not teachin' me anything. I'm going to be the boss in this family. Got that?'

Just then the dog barked at them, and she laughed.

'I agree with you, Blackie,' she said.

And when she moved to embrace Matt and kiss him, the sweetness of her lips turned him to mush, and he knew he was a goner.

THE END

Other titles in the
Linford Western Library:

THE CHISELLER

Tex Larrigan

Soon the paddle-steamer would be on its long journey down the Missouri River to St Louis. Now, all Saul Rhymer had to do was to play the last master-stroke of the evening. He looked at the mounting pile of gold and dollar bills and again at the cards in his hand. Then, looking around the table, he produced the deed to the goldmine in Montana. 'Let's play poker!' But little did he know how that journey back to St Louis would change his life so drastically.

THE ARIZONA KID

Andrew Mcbride

When former hired gun Calvin Taylor took the job of sheriff of Oxford County, New Mexico, it was for one reason only — to catch, or kill, the notorious Arizona Kid, and pick up the fifteen hundred dollars reward the governor had secretly offered. Taylor found himself on the trail of the infamous gang known as the Regulators, hunting down a man who'd once been his friend. The pursuit became, in every sense, a journey of death.

BULLETS IN BUZZARDS CREEK

Bret Rey

The discovery of a dead saloon girl is only the beginning of Sheriff Jeff Gilpin's problems. Fortunately, his old friend 'Doc' Holliday arrives in Buzzards Creek just as Gilpin is faced by an outlaw gang. In a dramatic shoot-out the sheriff kills their leader and Holliday's reputation scares the hell out of the others. But it isn't long before the outlaws return, when they know Holliday is not around, and Gilpin is alone against six men . . .

THE YANKEE HANGMAN

Cole Rickard

Dan Tate was given a virtually impossible task: to save the murderer Jack Williams from the condemned cell. Williams, scum that he was, held a secret that was dear to the Confederate cause. But if saving Williams would test all Dan's ingenuity, then his further mission called for immense courage and daring. His life was truly on the line and if he didn't succeed, Horace Honeywell, the Yankee Hangman would have the last word!

MISSOURI PALACE

S. J. Rodgers

When ex-lawman Jim Williams accepts the post of security officer on the *Missouri Palace* river-boat, he finds himself embroiled in a power struggle between Captain J. D. Harris and Jake Farrell, the murderous boss of Willow Flats, who will stop at nothing to add the giant sidepaddler to his fleet. Williams knows that with no one to back him up in a straight fight with Farrell's hired killers, he must hit them first and hit them hard to get out alive.